Anger sm~~~~~
Ludo~~

He came ~~~~~
tread, wh~~~~~~~~~~~~~~~~~~ of a
jungle cat ~~~~~~~~ stood together, so close
Krista could feel his breath on her face, and
she was very conscious that her heart was
hammering painfully against her ribs.

Before she knew what was happening he
had reached out, pulling her against him,
gazing down into her face with a dominating
expression. Krista, prepared to respond when
his mouth sought hers, gave way to the
familiar licking fire that his touch inevitably
inspired.

But the mouth that could be so gentle, so
persuasive, had abandoned tenderness and
right now sought only to subdue....

**Harlequin Romances
by Alexandra Scott**

2506 – LOVE ME AGAIN
2514 – THIS SIDE OF HEAVEN
2554 – CATCH A STAR
2585 – LOVE COMES STEALING
2604 – BORROWED GIRL

These books may be available at your local bookseller.

For a free catalog listing all titles currently available,
send your name and address to:

Harlequin Reader Service
P.O. Box 52040, Phoenix, AZ 85072-9988
Canadian address: Stratford, Ontario N5A 6W2

Borrowed Girl

Alexandra Scott

Harlequin Books

TORONTO • NEW YORK • LONDON
AMSTERDAM • PARIS • SYDNEY • HAMBURG
STOCKHOLM • ATHENS • TOKYO • MILAN

Original hardcover edition published in 1983
by Mills & Boon Limited

ISBN 0-373-02604-8

Harlequin Romance first edition February 1984

CHAPTER ONE

'WHY don't you leave the old trout and come away with me?'

Remembering his words, Krista gave a sleepy smile as she snuggled down even deeper under the duvet. She had been so shocked by his outrageous suggestion that evening when they had met at Aunt Diana's reception—so shocked that he had widened his eyes in a mocking parody of her own reaction before smiling, that intimate, professionally charming smile that had made her heart turn over completely. And that was how it had begun.

'Don't look so reproachful, Miss Ewing. I promise I'm perfectly serious when I ask you to come away with me.'

Krista had blushed, touching the tray she was holding in her right hand with her left to counteract any tendency to tremble. 'Oh, I couldn't possibly, Mr Hasek.' Glancing up at him through the long thick lashes which made such a seductive fringe for her grey eyes, she wondered if his keen ear had heard the betraying quiver in her voice. 'The old trout, as you describe her, depends on me completely.' And with what she hoped was a cool little smile she turned away to offer a glass of champagne and have a brief word with the newly arrived Lord Provost.

All the most important citizens of Edinburgh had been invited that evening to meet Ludovic Hasek, who had just arrived in the city for the series of orchestral concerts at which he was to be guest conductor. Lady James, Krista's Aunt Diana, was not the sort to allow such a coup to pass unnoticed, and she had made sure that the guest list was long and impressive. Even she had been surprised and obviously gratified that most of the invitations had been accepted instantly, at the same time allowing herself a little grumble that they would be forced to allow the guests to overflow from the large drawing room into the garden, but Krista knew her well enough to understand that the complaints were merely a cloak for her deep satisfaction. For after all, what could be a more positive confirmation of her place at the very summit of Edinburgh society?

Aunt Diana was a snob—only a little one and touchingly transparent in all her small vanities, but as far as her niece by marriage was concerned she was a minor tyrant as well. It had suited Lady James to provide a home for Krista after her parents had died, since it afforded her the opportunity not only to use her as a favourite dogsbody, but gave her the chance of a little showing off as well.

'She's Colin's niece really,' she would explain to any new acquaintance. 'Goodness knows what would have happened to her if we hadn't ...' She would sigh, and after sending Krista off on some invented errand would roll her eyes expressively at her visitors. 'Poor Morton was very improvident, and when he died Jean, Krista's mother, was left very badly off. Life was a struggle for her, and then when she was killed by that hit-and-run driver when Krista was only seventeen ...' The next sigh was usually accompanied by a shrug. 'Of course, Colin was devoted to his sister and to Krista as well so there was no question but that we should look after her. And I consider it a sacred trust to carry on where he left off.' Gently she would touch her eyes with a tiny lace hankie before smiling bravely at her sympathetic listeners. 'Of course, if we had ever had any children of our own things might have been different, but as it is ... Colin used always to say, if you can't have what you like then you must like what you have, and I've always tried to live by that philosophy.'

Krista, who had heard various parts of this speech at different times during the seven years she had lived with her aunt, found that gradually the hurt caused by the implications had softened until at last the only emotion engendered was mild amusement. Especially when she wondered if her aunt's tame guests ever considered how very easy it would be to like what Lady James had, the philosophy in which she took so much ingenuous pride.

Certainly the life she lived would seem to most people very comfortable indeed, in her large stone-built mansion with its view of Arthur's Seat, her few loyal middle-aged servants who ran the house with such impeccable efficiency and maintained the garden so that it was a joy to the eye at most seasons of the year.

Added to that the very comfortable income her husband had left for her sole use, the status conferred by his acquired title, the absorbing interest she had in the musical life of the capital, complete freedom to follow any whim she might have, and it would seem to the most exacting observer that such a life would be difficult indeed to dislike.

At least that was how it always seemed to Krista. The only thing that could be a possible lack was the companionship of her husband. And there were times when, rather ignobly, the girl

wondered if her darling Uncle Colin had been as
badly missed by his widow as he deserved to be.
Oh, Aunt Diana went through all the motions,
satisfied the casual onlooker, but it occurred to
Krista that the mantle of widowhood sat very
easily on Lady James's shoulders, that at the age
of fifty-five she found herself where all her life she
had longed to be—rich, a figure of some
consequence in her own circle and with no one to
please but herself.

Not that Krista was so censorious where her
aunt was concerned, because on the whole they got
on well enough together. Possibly the arrangement
suited them both, although there were times when
the girl longed to get away from the claustrophobic
atmosphere of Traquhair Lodge into the less
protected life enjoyed by ordinary girls of her own
age. But the only occasion when she had done
anything about it had been just before Uncle Colin
became ill, and his subsequent death shelved her
tentative inclination to stretch her wings. Then,
later, when she had felt able to bring up the
subject again, her aunt's reaction had been so
severe that she had reluctantly abandoned the idea
for ever.

'How can you think of abandoning me, Krista?'
As always Lady James was able to shed a few tears
at will. 'Just when I need you most! I don't . . . I
simply don't know what your uncle would have
thought!'

'But when I mentioned it before he didn't . . .'

'I'm sure if he'd known what was going to
happen, he would have been comforted by the idea
that I wouldn't be entirely alone. So . . . I'm to be
left in this great house with no one . . .' She waved
a dramatic hand round the elegant drawing-room,
her mouth trembling in self-pity. And she sighed

deeply. Lady James had always relied deeply on the sigh as an indication of emotions beyond words.

And it didn't seem the right moment for Krista to draw her aunt's attention to the fact that she had two servants living in, Mrs Meikle the housekeeper and John Lucas the gardener who had a small flat over the garage, besides a whole brigade of women who came daily to do the cleaning. So Krista merely gave way, acknowledging that at twenty-three she was condemned to live this kind of safe comfortable life for ever. Her only opportunity of changing would be if she married someone like Iain Melville who proposed to her at regular intervals or Hamish McGregor who she imagined wouldn't be averse to marrying the niece of Sir Colin James.

But it wouldn't be much of a change in either case. When she thought coldly, calmly and in great detail about what marriage entailed, introducing first Iain and then Hamish to these imaginary situations, she felt not the slightest throb of anything approaching excitement. In fact the only thought that came into her mind was a saying of Uncle Colin's when he wanted to describe something particularly unappealing: Like a plate of cold porridge without the salt. That just about summed up her feelings in relation to marriage with Iain and Hamish. Acceptable only in the last resort. So she might just as well stay where she was and put up with Aunt Diana's little foibles.

Which made it all the more surprising when just a week after Ludovic Hasek made his outrageous suggestion at her aunt's reception Krista flew off with him to Budapest. More unexpected still that Lady James, who had been so insistent that she could not manage without her niece-cum-social secretary, was a positive encouragement, a catalyst in this uncharacteristic course of action.

The very first time Krista had seen Ludovic Hasek had been at one of the concerts at the previous year's festival. She couldn't remember which orchestra he had been conducting, seeing so many tended to make them merge a bit after a while, but there was never any tendency to confuse him with any other conductor. There was only one Hasek, a fact that was as apparent to Krista as to her aunt, who kept repeating that particular piece of information until the girl felt she could scream.

'And he's so utterly charming.' Lady James, oblivious of her niece's reaction, went on as she sipped her morning coffee in the corner of the conservatory overlooking the lily pond. 'Such a pity you couldn't meet him, dear, but this meeting was strictly for committee. But,' she wrinkled her short nose girlishly, 'I did have a chance to speak a few private words to him and found that he's to be in Edinburgh several times next year, and I'm already planning something. I told him all about myself. He was *so* interested.' The sigh was tragic. 'I told him how I'd had to give up my career in music because I couldn't leave my parents.'

Krista appeared to listen to the old tale dutifully. It was true that her aunt had a pleasant voice, but whether she could have had a career as a concert singer was another matter. In fact Sir Colin had once, quite unconscious that he was letting the cat out of the bag, told Krista that they married prematurely simply because Diana wanted to get away from the dreary conventionality of life in a Fife manse.

'And he told me,' Lady James, unaware of any lack of attention, went on, 'that I may have given more pleasure as an amateur than as a professional.

Sometimes, he said, sometimes the amateur can bring freshness, the lighter approach to a performance that a professional lacks, and the human voice more than other instruments is a frail delicate thing, so easily damaged by over-exertion.

Krista smiled at that, for it was very difficult to think of her aunt as anything but robust; words like frail and delicate were the very last that would occur when thinking of her. But deep down was a slight quiver of anticipation that perhaps when he returned to Edinburgh next year she might have the opportunity to speak to the great conductor.

When that time arrived Krista had met him once or twice casually, being introduced briefly by her aunt and then ignored by both while they became involved with the plans and discussions that were the concerns of the sub-committee. Krista, because of her connection of such a generous patron of the arts as Lady James, was usually given the task of taking notes and generally undertaking jobs which no one else wanted. As a rule she didn't mind this, but there were times, such as this one in the presence of Mr Hasek, when her aunt's off hand manner rankled a little.

'Krista, you can see to that, can't you? There was that little man in the Haymarket who printed our special invitations so nicely last time. Krista is so good at talking to these people.' The way she smiled round the table indicated that such mundane matters were too boring for someone like herself.

Glancing up from her notebook into which she was hurriedly scribbling the conflicting instructions that issued from those sitting round the table, the girl found Ludovic Hasek looking at her with a strange expression in his eyes. And to begin with they were such strange, such unexpectedly strange eyes. For who would have expected a man like that, a man with such black hair, such olive skin, to have eyes of that particular intense blue. Their depth of colour made the whites especially brilliant for just an instant before a flick of thick dark lashes concealed whatever he might have been thinking.

For what seemed a long time Krista looked at the handsome impassive features, unaware that her fingers holding the pen had tightened into a fierce grip but only too uncomfortably conscious of the rapid beating of her heart against the wall of her chest, a sensation that was halfway between choking and some totally incomprehensible excitement. For some reason she couldn't explain she felt vague dissatisfaction that she was wearing an old blouse. When she had put it on this morning it had seemed entirely suitable, but now her mind kept hankering after the new one in her wardrobe. It was in a soft rose pink, highly flattering, and would hardly have been out of place.

'Krista!' From the way her aunt spoke it was patently obvious that she was speaking for the second, maybe even for the third time. Amused impatience at her niece's daydreaming accompanied smiling exasperation in that swift glance round the table. 'Have you got that? Mrs Dalrymple-Shand would like you to go and pick up some packages from the station and take them direct to her house.'

'Very well.' Trying to ignore the flame of colour in her cheeks, Krista scribbled again in her notebook, but was relieved when she looked across to find Ludovic Hasek gathering up his papers while chatting and laughing with the person sitting next to him.

There had been a similar meeting just a few days later, one at which the conductor's presence had been entirely unexpected, merely a quick dash in and out while he had a hasty discussion with the chairman to clarify one or two points. Krista shrank back in her seat, anxious to escape his notice, and was convinced she had done so until he sauntered towards the door, talking intensely with Mr Forbes while the disturbing eyes rested on Krista's face, giving the impression that he wasn't really seeing her.

That was why his sudden, entirely mischievous suggestion on the day of the reception had been so much of a shock. Krista had convinced herself that he wasn't even aware of her existence, more important to her self-esteem that he hadn't noticed Lady James's slightly autocratic manner when speaking to her niece. But then Aunt Diana had summoned her over to offer him a drink from the silver tray she was carrying.

'Krista, Mr Hasek hasn't a drink.'

'I'm . . . I'm sorry.' Even the knowledge that she was wearing a particularly attractive dress wasn't enough to guarantee the assurance she would have liked to deal with the situation, and she blushed as she held out the glasses towards them.

'Thank you.' His voice was deep and vibrant, the accent transatlantic but with enough of his native Hungarian remaining to make it very intriguing. She glanced up as he raised the glass in an almost imperceptible salute to her before taking it to his lips and she had the quite ridiculous feeling that he was finding something about the situation amusing and absurd.

Before there was any opportunity for conversation her aunt was called away by the arrival of some other guests, and that was when he said what he did.

'Why don't you leave the old trout and come away with me?' The brilliant eyes narrowed slightly as he gazed down at her before mocking with the parody of her reactions and smiling that devastating smile.

Krista had positively wrenched her eyes from his, following the short dumpy figure of her aunt as she shook hands with the newcomers. A flicker of hysteria started into life as it occurred to her that the description was too accurate for comfort. Aunt Diana had chosen to wear a dress in a silvery material not dissimilar to fish scales, and it fitted almost as closely as a skin. But then she decided he had no right whatsoever to be making jokes at his hostess's expense, and that was when she had turned away with her cool little disclaimer.

After that first fraught encounter she determined that her manner towards him would be correct but distant, only she wouldn't have admitted that she was deliberately avoiding the most important guest. It was just that he was so much in demand, such a big fish, she told herself with a faint inward smile at the extension of the metaphor, that he wouldn't be interested in a minnow like herself.

And besides, it gave her the opportunity of paying a bit of extra attention to Iain Melville. Her conscience told her she had been neglecting him recently, and it would be a long time before she had such an ideal opportunity for making it up to him.

It was only when she noticed the slightly bemused look in Iain's eyes that it occurred to her that perhaps she had overdone it and that she would have to prepare to deflect another proposal. But at that very moment of realisation she looked up and found Ludovic Hasek's eyes on her, so she returned her attention to what Iain was saying, feigned fascinated interest, although she had no idea what he was talking about. From the corner of her eye she could see that he was still lounging with one elbow on the open top of the grand piano, taking with Jane McDonald who was hanging on to each word that he spoke and smiling with her usual vivacity.

Krista felt an unaccustomed pang of annoyance. Usually she was able to laugh at Jane's man-hungry attitude, although it was something she had found hard to understand. Why should a girl like Jane who as far as one could judge had everything to recommend her have to try so hard to attract the attention of every man who came into her orbit? She had the kind of looks, long blonde hair, fair skin and blue eyes, that should have had men clustering round her and the kind of fame that made her name a household word, and yet . . .

'I see Jane's trying to snare the lion.' Iain's dry remark brought Krista's eyes back to his face, consciously trying to subdue the colour that his words brought to her cheeks. She hadn't wanted her interest in the two beside the piano to be so obvious.

'Yes.' Casually rising to her feet, she held out a hand to him. 'Shall we go and have a walk round the garden? I promised to help with the supper, and if we don't go now . . .' Deliberately she allowed him to retain her hand in his until they had passed Ludovic Hasek, but she withdrew it as they walked through the french window into the garden.

But that didn't stop Iain, who probably thought he had received enough encouragement to justify his actions in pulling her against him when they reached the concealing shelter of the high rhododendrons which marked the edge of the formal part of the garden.

'Iain, no!'

But her protest had no effect, for his mouth had closed on hers with more than his usual possessiveness and Krista resorted to her normal reaction of remaining totally passive in his arms. She even kept her eyes open, trying to distract her thoughts from the rather tedious present experience by watching a late bee buzzing heavily about a perfect full blown pink rose. Eventually Iain noticed her lack of response and his arms slackened so that she was able to step out of his embrace.

'I said *no*, Iain.' Refusing to look at him, she put up a finger to touch one of the blossoms.

'You say no, but you act yes.' His tone was stiff and angry.

For a moment Krista's eyes flicked towards him, guiltily conscious that there was some truth in his words. 'Just because I try to be pleasant to my aunt's . . .'

'I'm not one of your aunt's guests, so don't say that, Krista. You know, or if you don't then you ought to know, that I don't come to these shindigs to please Lady James. I don't give a damn for her, and all I want is to get you away from all this.' He gave a brief glance back over his shoulder towards the house. 'But I suppose it's a lot to give up. I can't offer you the kind of life to which you've obviously become accustomed.'

'Oh, Iain!' The injustice of this stung Krista into defending herself. 'That's not fair! And it isn't true—you must know that.'

'Do I?' For once he wasn't to be cajoled into agreeing with her. 'Oh, I don't mean just the money, although an ordinary lawyer isn't going to be able to compete, but I can see that there are other things.' His pause was meaningful. 'You're dazzled by the people you meet—all these important visitors you see at Festival time. I hate to watch you losing your head over it all, Krista.' His tight-lipped tone echoed the contempt which many of his fellow citizens felt for the arty-crafty, but his next comment really stung. 'You couldn't keep your eyes off that conductor fellow in there.'

'How dare you!' Krista fairly shouted the words at him at the same instant as her hand came up in an arc and struck him on the cheek. The slap caused her fingers to sting and four prominent stripes were almost instantly visible on Iain's smooth cheek. Shattered by what was such a totally out of character reaction, Krista stared at him, noticing the flush of anger in his fair skin, the dark angry streaks of red on his right cheek where her fingers had struck with such force. It was a moment before either of them spoke, but he was the first to do so, depriving her of the opportunity to apologise.

'Well, at least that's clear enough. I'm sorry I've troubled you for so long, but I think I've got the message at last. Goodbye, Krista.' And with that he turned away, and she stood miserably watching the tall stockily built figure striding along the path. From the route he took she knew that he had no intention of going through the house again but was leaving by a gate in the garden wall. It seemed pointless to try to stop him, and the only regret she had was that she had acted so foolishly earlier in the evening. Iain's accusation was justified.

She *had* acted yes while she had said no. And it was degrading to think that she had slapped his face—so hard too. She could still hear the echo of it in her ears. A faint sob escaped her lips and she

sank down on to the garden seat, desperately
trying to control her inclination to cry.

She couldn't have said just when she became
aware of the scent of tobacco in her nostrils, but
when she realised that someone was smoking a
cigar quite close to her, she got up at once from
her seat and blew her nose, quietly but firmly so
that she had the chance of pulling herself together
before she emerged from the protection of the
bushes.

The faintly glowing end of his cigar among the
dusky shadows betrayed his position immediately,
and Krista drew in a breath when she realised that
Ludovic Hasek was lounging against a gate just
behind where she had had her brief scene with
Iain. She had no time to wonder if he had heard,
because the expression on his face told her at once
that he had.

'Miss Ewing.' He stepped towards her, his eyes
narrowing slightly as if she were some particularly
interesting specimen, noticing her heightened
colour, the faint trembling of her lips which no
amount of biting was able to control totally.

'Mr Hasek.' The best form of defence was
attack, but that was not her justification for her
immediate sharp reaction. 'Do you make a habit
of listening to other people's private conversa-
tions?' It wasn't the kind of smart crushing
comment she would have liked to make, but the
words came to her lips before she had the chance
to select them. Her mind was feverishly absorbed
by the worry of what he might have heard. Iain
had accused her of being unable to keep her eyes
off . . . Oh, God, could he have heard that?

'No.' His voice was colder than she remembered
it. 'Not as a rule.'

That meant he had heard. What she hoped was

a glare was spoiled by the blurry wetness of her eyes so she had no choice but to turn abruptly away from him, but before she could move, his fingers had caught her wrist, pulling her back towards him.

'Don't go yet, Miss Ewing.' His voice had regained all its potent charm. 'Tell me about the house.' Holding her arm securely, he guided her along the path that led them away from the house. 'How old is it? What is its style?'

'It's what they call Scottish baronial.' Krista answered his questions without really thinking about them, responding as he kept up a casual conversation while they did a complete circuit of the garden, returning to where the crowds were spilling on to the terrace.

'Now,' at last he released his grip on her arm, turning so that they faced each other, 'your aunt despatched me to fetch you. It seems your services are required in the kitchen.' He spoke as if she ought to resent such demands, but she was too involved with his first remark to absorb the implication of the second. Her aunt had sent him and . . .

'I'm sorry, Mr Hasek.' It couldn't be helped that her cheeks were scarlet with embarrassment. 'I was rude to you.'

'Think nothing of it.' There was something about a smile like his, thought Krista, trying not to watch his mouth. 'Think nothing of it, my dear Miss Ewing. I've been known to be rude myself from time to time and I trust my friends to forgive me. Only,' his hand came out to touch her face with a gentle finger, tracing the curve of her cheek in a way that brought a distinct tremor to the base of her spine, 'if life becomes too difficult for you, remember what I said to you earlier this evening.'

She was trying to drag her eyes from his face, struggling to remember exactly what he had said to her, when the sound of her aunt's voice calling her name made her jerk round towards the french windows. The old trout. Aunt Diana in her tight silver lamé dress was hurrying towards them across the terrace, her dark eyebrows pulled together in a distracted way.

'Krista!' Then discretion edged the impatience from her voice, her face cleared as she smiled brilliantly at the tall dark man. 'Thank you so much for finding her, Mr Hasek. So clever of you! Now, dear, Amy has been asking for you for simply ages. If you could just run in and help them, I know how grateful they would be.'

'Of course, Aunt. Excuse me, Mr Hasek.' She hardly dared look at him for fear the flicker of amusement she was trying to subdue should find a reflection in his eyes but simply turned and walked quickly into the house, really rather grateful for the opportunity to busy herself with the hundred and one things which needed some attention. And she took great care that she avoided Ludovic Hasek for the rest of the evening.

And he didn't go out of his way to seek her out—which should have pleased her but strangely didn't. Neither did the conversation she overheard when she hurried past the corner where he was eating supper with Jane McDonald.

'And how is it, Jane, that I haven't seen you on television?'

'I suppose,' Jane's speaking voice was as seductive as her singing, 'I suppose it's because you haven't been looking for me. Perhaps now,' Krista could imagine long fingers being placed on his dark sleeve, eyes narrowing invitingly, in fact the entire battery of the McDonald props being brought into action, 'perhaps now you *will* look.'

And Ludovic Hasek's deep laugh told Krista more certainly than anything else would have done, that this was a game whose rules he knew only too well. It was easy for her to sweep some dirty crockery up in one hand and take them off to the kitchen in a gesture that was meant to pour scorn on both of them. And for the rest of the evening while she threw herself into the domestic chores she reassured herself that she would hate to be like Jane. Quite convinced herself.

Until, after the last guest had gone, when the last crystal goblet had been polished and replaced in its cupboard, the last silver knife burnished and laid carefully in its velvet-lined box, she was at last free to go to her bedroom.

And then as she lay in momentary exhaustion on the closed door, the ache in her chest grew until it almost choked her and she admitted she had been kidding herself. She wouldn't hate to be like Jane—not in the very least. In fact she would much rather be Jane McDonald than Krista Ewing. Who wouldn't?

She thrust herself away from the door, moving listlessly towards the huge wardrobe with the long bevelled mirror where she stood surveying her reflection. The dress she was wearing, which she had really liked when she had chosen it last week, now presented a totally different appearance. The colour, a soft flattering pink, still appealed to her, but there was something wrong with the style. And she could only conclude that her change of mind had something to do with the dazzling black and gold dress, a short swirly kind of thing made in some fine sort of material, which Jane McDonald had been wearing.

On her, of course, it looked stunning, a complete foil for her colouring, but entirely unsuitable for someone less sophisticated. Someone like me, Krista decided without enthusiasm, although it was hard to decide exactly where her own looks went wrong. Individually all her features were reasonable enough, it was the sum of the parts that was so unimpressive.

She was a reasonable height, slender if not exactly willowy. Deep grey eyes which she had been told were unusual with her dark gold hair. But it was Uncle Colin who had made that comparison, and she could hardly deny that he was biased. He hadn't been able to find any excuse for her mouth, which was quite definitely on the large side, so that she had to try to remember not to grin when something funny happened. Usually she forgot until it was too late, so that was no good, only her teeth were unusually white and perhaps that made up.

She ought to be thankful for having such good teeth, she decided as she moved away from the mirror with a sigh of despair, for even Jane had had to have something done about hers when she first started on television. Krista remembered a time when Jane's teeth had been crooked and not very white, but suddenly all that changed and she had gone about dazzling all her acquaintances with that perfect white smile, a great tribute to the miracles of modern dentistry.

Suddenly the idea that physical weaknesses, blemishes even weren't something that had to be endured for ever seemed immensely cheering, and Krista began to sing faintly as she turned down the covers of her bed. She didn't really wish she were Jane McDonald. Not even if she were on the threshold of an affair with Ludovic Hasek. For she was very much afraid, and this *was* an irredeemable flaw, that she would want only one man, with no diversions along the way. Only one man. And she must try to be patient until she found him, this one man in the world who would love her for herself alone.

For the next three days Krista scarcely thought of Ludovic Hasek at all. It took all the concentration she possessed to guide her thoughts along deliberate paths unconnected with music or the Festival or any of the things which usually absorbed her aunt and herself, but by sheer will-power she was able to do it. There was one uneasy moment while she was opening the dozens of thank-you letters which arrived in the days following the party and which she passed across the breakfast table unread. The sight of bold black handwriting on a thick white envelope gave her a little quiver, it was so obviously not the kind of script taught in Scottish schools. Or in English, she decided as she hastily added it to the pile. There was something foreign and confident about it, it might even have been ostentantious if it hadn't been for the aggressive masculinity of the strong flowing lines.

'Hmm.' Her aunt's happy little exclamation as she took it from the top of the heap, the curve of her lips, confirmed Krista's suspicions. Her reaction to a thank-you from a mere Lord Provost or a Moderator of the General Assembly would have been gratified but restrained, with none of the skittish blushing confusion Ludovic Hasek's letter caused.

'I shall be going out this afternoon, Krista.' Impatiently she pushed aside the unread letters. 'I think I'm supposed to be going to a committee meeting at the hospital, so telephone and cancel it for me, will you, dear.' She hardly waited for Krista's murmur of agreement before she returned to the letter she was still holding. 'So charming of the dear boy! There's something that only I can help him with, he says. Disaster has struck.' She laughed. 'How dramatic! I'm quite certain it's nothing, but I must do as he suggests and have tea with him this afternoon. Curiosity will force me to go if nothing else. Oh, and he does say he sends his best wishes to dear Miss Ewing. Isn't that kind of him, Krista? To remember you.' Becoming aware of the silence, she raised her head to look at her niece with a half exasperated expression. 'Ludovic Hasek I'm talking about, Krista. But I'll leave you to deal with all the letters. I'll try to find time to go through them all later, but now,' she pushed back her chair and walked to the door of the small morning room where they had their meals when they were alone, 'now I must make a telephone call.' She was singing happily as she crossed the hall in the direction of the telephone room.

Krista felt a vague nagging pain all that day and tried to remember what she had eaten to cause her to have indigestion. It wasn't a complaint she had experienced before, but the symptoms seemed indisputable, and the fact that Mrs Meikle's favourite remedy failed to ease the discomfort could only be put down to beginner's bad luck. The housekeeper's second choice of a long walk across the park had been slightly more effective, and when Krista returned to Traquhair Lodge just after five in the afternoon she was feeling a bit better.

'Her Ladyship wants to see you at once, Krista. In the library.' Mrs Meikle met her in the hall with the instructions, screwing up her face as she sometimes did when she wanted to give a message without actually speaking. 'Are you feeling any better, lass?' she asked belatedly.

'I'm fine now.' Krista hung up her raincoat in the cloakroom and with the briefest of pauses to ensure that her hair was tidy enough she walked over to the door of the library. It was only when she was turning the handle that she heard her aunt's special gurgling laugh and knew that she had someone with her, but she didn't imagine it could possibly be Ludovic Hasek. Not till the door was pushed open did it occur to her that her aunt might have brought him back from their rendez-vous, and his face bent over the scrapbook which he was sharing with Lady James confirmed the idea the moment it flashed into her mind.

Almost at once he looked up at her, one swift keen glance taking in the plain style of her dress, the way her hair was pulled back behind her ears in a not particularly becoming way. *And* doubtless gratified that colour was staining her cheeks. She turned to close the door to hide her momentary confusion, feeling she was more under control by the time she faced them again.

'Miss Ewing.' He had risen to his feet, tall and graceful in pale grey slacks and black turtleneck sweater under a brown leather jacket.

'Good afternoon, Mr Hasek.' God, she thought, how prim and middle-aged I sound! How amusing he must find us. Upset by the discerning expression in his eyes, she turned to smile at her aunt, correctly interpreting the book which rested on her knee. 'Have you been showing off your cuttings, Aunt Diana?'

'Yes. Ludovic has been so interested.'

Krista flicked an enquiring glance at the man who still appeared to find contemplation of her face an absorbing interest. Certainly there was nothing in his expression to suggest that he had found it unutterably boring.

'But although we were looking at my pictures.' There was something so coy and kittenish about her aunt's tone that Krista looked at her curious to hear what was coming next, 'We were talking about you Krista.'

'About me?' Suspiciously she looked from one to the other, then smiled selfconsciously. 'Why should you have been talking about me?'

Lady James laughed softly before she put down her book and eased herself from the deep settee where she and Ludovic had been sitting. Daringly she slipped her hand into his arm and smiled coquettishly up at him. 'Shall you tell her, Ludovic? Or shall I?'

His eyes lingered for a moment longer on Krista's then with a tiny shrug, a faint smile, he looked down at his hostess. All at once Krista was aware that the terrible discomfort had come back into her chest and this time it was accompanied by a loud throbbing in her ears, a clammy dampness on the palms of her hands. She could not imagine what they were going to tell her and . . . she dared not allow herself to imagine.

The noise in her ears cleared a little, the pain eased from her chest when he took a step towards her, a faintly anxious expression on his face. 'Are you all right, Krista?' His strange foreign accent seemed to show some concern and the fingers he put out to touch hers were sympathetic.

'I'm perfectly all right.' Her laugh sounded normal enough. 'Just dying with curiosity, that's all.' Coolly she withdrew her hand from his, walked over to the fireplace and sat down in one of the chintz-covered easy-chairs.

'Well, I know you'll be pleased, Krista, although

it will be such a change for you at first.' Despite
the smile which she kept firmly fixed on her lips
Krista felt the squeezing pain tighten round her.
'The truth of it is, dear, that Ludovic is in a
desperate jam, and it seems as if you're the only
one who can help him solve it. His secretary has
had to go back to Hungary because of a family
emergency, his father is quite seriously ill, and at
short notice it's impossible to find a suitable
replacement. So we've arranged, he and I,' she sat
down, then patted the seat beside her encouragingly, 'that he can borrow you for three months,
and you're to fly off to Budapest with him next
week!'

Krista was scarcely aware of the slackening, the
release of the tight band around her heart, nor the
sudden quieting of all her excited pulses. She was
too busy trying to cope with the unexpected surge
of anger that began deep down inside and frothed
up in an instantaneous tide. Her eyes flashed at
him, leaving him in no doubt of her reactions, and
the faint narrowing of his gaze told her that he had
not mistaken the message. She took a long deep
breath, determined that this time she would find
the right words, words which would leave him in
no doubt as to her opinion, but before they could
be formulated her aunt's bright voice chipped in
again.

'There Ludovic, I told you so. She's so thrilled
that she doesn't know what to say to you!'

'Oh, but you're wrong, Aunt.' Krista's voice was
at its sweetest, its most reasonable. 'My breath was
taken away for just a moment. But now,' in
Ludovic's direction she smiled her wide, white
smile, 'now I've had a moment to think about it I
know exactly what I'm going to say to Mr Hasek.'
She took a deep breath.

CHAPTER TWO

BUT before she could speak the door opened and Mrs Meikle came into the room. 'I'm sorry, Your Ladyship, I know you said you didn't want any calls, but Sir John Graeme is on the telephone and he's most insistent that he speaks to you now. I told him you were engaged, but . . .'

'Oh dear!' Lady James was only slightly annoyed, but she sighed heavily as she levered herself from the settee. 'These people are so self-important that they don't consider others in any way. If you'll excuse me for a few moments, Ludovic. Anyway,' she spoke over her shoulder as she walked to the door, 'you'll be able to explain all about your flights and so on.'

The door closed behind her and silence enveloped the two who were looking at each other with such intensity. At once all the carefully-chosen words slipped out of Krista's mind and others she hadn't until then even thought of burst from her lips.

'You've a damned cheek, I must say!' She was slightly shocked by her own impetuosity, but impressed too.

'Have I?' Still looking at her, he reached into an inside pocket and pulled out a cigarette case. 'Do you mind if I smoke?' Without waiting for an answer he put the cigarette between his lips and flicked a light to it.

'Do you care?'

His eyebrows were raised questioningly, but before he could say anything Krista hurried on.

'You ask my permission but don't trouble to wait for an answer!'

'You are quite right, of course. Forgive me.' He went forward to a side table where a large crystal ashtray winked impressively, but before he could stub out the end she perversely stopped him. 'Of course I don't mind you smoking. I told you what I objected to. And as well you assume that I don't smoke.'

'Right again.' He shrugged philosophically, stepping towards her again while he fished in his pocket for the case. 'Would you care to smoke, Miss Ewing?'

Although the eyes were as impassive as ever she had the feeling that he was laughing at her; perhaps guessing that she didn't smoke, he was anticipating her confusion.

'Thank you.' She took and put one into her mouth and sat waiting for the small flame to be applied to the end, then drew the smoke into her mouth, holding it there for a moment before exhaling, as slowly as her bursting lungs could achieve. Her eyes stung, but she looked at him with cool disdain.

'Now, Miss Ewing.' He leaned against the mantelpiece, watching her closely. 'Or may I call you Krista?'

She nodded, and conscious of the expectant look on his face she puffed again at the cigarette, blushing crimson when he was unable to hide his amusement any longer.

'Give it to me. Please.' He took it from her and quickly extinguished it in the ashtray. 'Really,' his mouth was still curved into a smile and she thought how wonderful his teeth looked against the darkness of his skin, 'really it does not suit you, Krista.' The way he spoke her name, with that attractive rolling of the consonant, made that little flicker of emotion stir disturbingly again. 'You look ... quite different with a cigarette between your lips.'

She thought it best to ignore that and returned to the first thing in her mind but with less belligerence than before. 'About this mad idea, Mr Hasek ...'

'I'm sorry you heard it as you did. It was not ... tactful of your aunt to tell you as if it had all been arranged without you.'

'And hadn't it?'

'Of course not.'

'It sounded remarkably like it to me. You are to borrow me,' her smile was meant to be sarcastic, 'and presumably my aunt is going to lend me. For three months! Just as if I were some old umbrella she could do without!' The smile faded and she bit her lip to stifle a sob which had unexpectedly crept up on her.

'Let's say no more about it, shall we?' He strode over to the table and ground out his cigarette with suppressed anger. 'It's clear enough that the idea is one that you dislike.' He turned round and faced her, his eyes seeming to scorch contemptuously over her so that immediately she had the feeling of lost opportunity, but before she had time to think of any reply the door opened again and her aunt came into the room protesting mildly over what Sir John Graeme had said to her on the telephone.

She was comfortably ensconced in her seat again when the strain in the atmosphere percolated through to her, and she looked from one to the other in questioning bewilderment. 'Is it all right?' She laughed lightly. 'I suppose, Krista, you were taken completely by surprise. Such a wonderful opportunity must have been the last thing you expected.'

'I think, Lady James,' all Ludovic Hasek's annoyance had left him, he was once more his urbane controlled self, 'perhaps we have taken Miss Ewing's reaction for granted.'

Quite unreasonably Krista was hurt by that 'Miss Ewing' more than by anything he was likely to say.

'Of course we haven't!' Lady James laughed at the mere idea. 'What girl in her right mind wouldn't jump at such a chance? And,' she turned from Ludovic to her niece who was sitting opposite her, 'Krista really is a very amenable child as a rule. Tell me, dear,' encouragingly she leaned forward, her elbow on her knee, 'don't you feel excited at the prospect of seeing so many wonderful new places?'

Only for a second did Krista hesitate, but then recollection of that sense of something precious slipping through her fingers struck her with renewed force and without looking once in the direction of Ludovic Hasek she answered the question with her usual quietness, quite as if that earlier outburst hadn't occurred. 'Very excited, Aunt Diana. I can still hardly believe it's happened.'

With unexpected emotion her aunt rose, rushed across the floor and embraced her. 'I'm so glad for you, Krista!' And looking over her aunt's shoulder Krista was not surprised to see a very perplexed smile touching the corner of the visitor's mouth.

'But now I must go and tell Mrs Meikle that we'll have one extra for dinner. No,' Lady James waved aside Ludovic Hasek's murmured protest, 'I won't listen to a refusal. We have so much to talk about, so many plans to be made.' Moments later the door closed once again.

Krista felt all her self-confidence suddenly

evaporate and she sat, her heart thumping loudly, looking at her hands folded in her lap. She heard a sigh, then from underneath her long lashes saw his figure slump down on the settee. 'I wish Lady James would allow one to decide things for oneself. Really there was something I wanted to do this evening.'

'Yes,' Krista raised her eyes, looking very innocently into his, 'isn't that exactly what I was saying?'

For a moment he glared at her, then he put back his head and laughed. *'Touché, ma petite!'* Still smiling, he shrugged his shoulders, then to her dismay he got up and came across to stand in front of her. Seconds later she was jerked to her feet by strong hands which refused to release her when she was standing facing him.

Her blood pressure increased a few points as his face came towards her, and he grinned when she jerked her head away from his. 'Don't be so nervous, Miss Ewing.' Krista wondered if he noticed the way her bosom was rising and falling—not with agitation because of his threatening attitude but with an excitement she was doing her damnedest to suppress. Suddenly, and to her relief, his grasp relaxed, although she could still feel the strength of his fingers when they had gone. But he was very close to her and she could not move back because of the chair against her legs.

'Are you always so perverse, Krista?' The tone of his voice turned her bones to water—and the touch of his hand! The touch of his hand when it came up to her cheek, trickling softly down her skin that she longed to jerk her head away as she had done before. Only this time she was helpless.

'Perverse?' She tried to inject some firmness, some matter-of-fact resolution into her voice, anything that would hide from him the melting betraying feelings his touch engendered. She tried, but was uncertain that she had succeeded.

'Yes, you are perverse, Krista.' He dropped his hand to his side and it was a relief to her when he moved away from her changing the subject completely. 'Now,' he glanced at the slim gold watch on his wrist, 'be a good girl and tell your aunt that I'm sorry I can't stay to dinner.' He crossed to the french window, turned the key in the lock and stepped outside on to the terrace, pausing for a moment in the half-open doorway. 'This is becoming like one of those Whitehall farces, with all the young men coming and going through the garden!'

It was a split second before the significance of this dawned on Krista; she remembered Iain's departure and the colour flowed into her cheeks, but before she could make an angry retort the main door opened suddenly and Lady James reappeared. Her expression when she looked at the two so close to the french window was surprised, but Ludovic stepped back into the room with a charming smile.

'Lady James, I've been trying to persuade Krista to show me the garden before I go.'

'Before you go?' Consternation was painfully obvious in every word.

'Yes—I'm so sorry. Had I known——!'He dealt himself a light but dramatic blow on the temple with a sidelong glance at Krista which Lady James could not see. 'I would so much rather have been dining here with Krista and yourself. But I promise that if you'll invite me another evening it will take wild horses to keep me away. Those or the Festival committee, of course. But you know exactly what my commitments are.'

'Oh, I'm so sorry.' Lady James was surprisingly mild in view of the chopping and changing of her meal arrangements. 'Then off you go, Krista, show Ludovic the garden. Although I would have thought you would have seen enough of it the other night. I didn't know you were so very keen.'

'There is so much that we don't know about each other, Lady James. But I hope that in time . . .' He clasped a hand firmly about Krista's arm, impelling her towards the door. 'If it hadn't been for this previous arrangement . . .'

'Oh, that's all right.' Lady James smiled graciously. 'I should have thought! Someone I know, is it?'

'Some old trout from the music world. Isn't that what you said to me?' Krista enquired sweetly, ignoring his frowning signals.

'Really, Krista, I can't believe . . .' Her eyes gleamed with curiosity. 'Oh, do tell me, Ludovic! Who on earth did you mean?'

'Lady James, I couldn't possibly tell you such a thing. Next time you confronted this . . . this person, you would be sure to feel terribly embarrassed.'

'Would I? How intriguing!'

A few moments later they had escaped, and still retaining his grasp on Krista's arm, Ludovic hurried her in the direction of the wall gate.

'You provoking little devil!' He ground the words at her through clenched teeth.

'You should have the courage of your convictions. You wanted me to leave the old trout. Now you seem to have achieved it. You ought to feel satisfied and not mind telling her what you think.'

Fiercely he swung her round to look at him. 'Do you really mean that? You would have been happy if she had known?'

'No.' Her voice was uncertain and she coloured guiltily. 'Of course I wouldn't. Only it was worth the risk to see you just a little bit disconcerted. You're too sure of yourself by half, Mr Hasek—much too used to having your own way in everything.'

'And you're not?' His hand dropped from her arm.

'Of course not!' Indignation, outraged indignation sounded in every syllable.

'Then it's high time you learned how, Miss Ewing.'

'And I'm sure I couldn't find a better teacher.' She was quite pleased with her instant response.

'My opinion exactly, Miss Ewing.' He smiled disturbingly. 'There are many things which I could teach you. And I find I'm more and more looking forward to the opportunity of doing so. *Ciao.*'

A moment later Krista was gazing at the green-painted surface of the wooden gate as it closed behind him.

Looking back on it afterwards, Krista could remember little about the remaining days in Edinburgh before she left on the plane with Ludovic. It was a blur of bewilderment in which the only things to stand out were the orgy of clothes buying, the two concerts where she went to watch him conduct and the endless reminders she had from Lady James about her great good fortune and the wonderful opportunity she had been presented with.

But the only time she saw much of Ludovic Hasek was the evening when he came to dine with them at Traquhair Lodge. It was an occasion Krista had looked forward to, had taken a great deal of trouble over her dress and make-up, so it was a disappointment to find that she was scarcely noticed. All the slightly mad teasing she had found so stimulating, had enjoyed so much, had gone. And it wasn't until she was standing in the hall, rather disconsolately saying goodnight, that he seemed to shake himself from his mood of abstraction and smile at her.

'Forgive me, Krista.' He grinned, that faintly devilish mocking smile she found so hard to resist. 'I have had worries about the Kodaly I am to conduct tomorrow night. I excuse the players who do not know the composer as I do, but all day we have practised and it goes not right.' For the first time since she had met him she noticed a tiny lapse in his English. 'You come to hear it tomorrow, *drágám*?'

'Yes.' The expression on his face made her blush, and she had no idea what the last word meant. 'I'm looking forward to it.'

'And so we must practise the more, to make it perfect for you. And I want to tell you . . .' His fingers came up to curl a strand of her hair, to brush against her cheek.

'This is what I was looking for, Ludovic.' Lady James, her voice expressing relief, came bustling in from the library, a slightly tattered piece of music in her hand. 'How annoyed I should have been if I'd been unable to find it! As I was saying, Colin and I used to sing this together before we were married.'

And they began to talk over the songbook, so Krista never heard what it was he had in his mind to tell her. And moments later he was bowing over her aunt's hand, sending her a mischievous look as he did the same with hers and said goodnight.

When she reached the bedroom she leaned back against the door for a moment, then walked forward to the dressing-table to examine her reflection wondering if she could find an answer to the vague feeling of disappointment which beset her. It was such a contrast to her expectations when she had left her room just a few hours earlier.

Then she had been high on the knowledge that she was looking better than she ever had before in her life. The soft subtle green of her dress and its style, cut high under the bust with a flowing skirt, was one that suited her. Of course it wasn't as attractive as some of her new ones, but these must be kept. Like a trousseau. She knew that her aunt would never approve of her using any of her new things before she even embarked on the reason for buying them. But the green dress had looked very nice, especially with her hair shining and hanging loose to her shoulders.

Her eyes too had been shining then, but they weren't now. They were dull and tired, she decided, with a yawn to excuse them. And she might just as well get ready for bed. She was silly to feel disappointed. After all, what did she expect? He was virtually her employer, wasn't he, and she needn't expect compliments and pretty speeches from him. Anyway, like most artists he would be much too self-absorbed to pay much attention to someone else. She had known too many of them to have any illusions on that score.

She was to find that prejudice confirmed all too forcibly in the weeks that followed, not simply as far as Ludovic was concerned, for she decided as she struggled with orders and requests in what seemed a dozen different languages that they were all equally arrogant, temperamental and inconsiderate. More than once she wondered, with a faint sense of desperation, just what she was doing, trailing all over Europe with a fanatic, however brilliant, when life could have been going along unexcitingly, uneventfully but comfortably at Traquhair Lodge.

But then there was the music. When she slumped down exhausted in the third row from the back where a few seats were always reserved for friends of the performers, and let the joy and beauty of it wash away all her cares and irritation. Those few fleeting moments she knew she would not exchange for any other experience she had ever had.

And the applause, in which she was such an enthusiastic participant. She shared it with him— although of course she wouldn't have dared to let him know that. She was a cog, the smallest cog imaginable in the machine, but part of it nonetheless, and the enthusiasm was intoxicating.

She would never forget the first night in Budapest. Finding herself so emotionally involved with the occasion owed everything to the music, the location, the conductor and the man. It had been moving to see him receive such an ovation when he walked on to the stage, bowing briefly, then to experience the total silence that waited for him to raise his baton, the sighing ecstasy as the Hungarian audience listened to the melancholy opening bars of the Dances of Galanta, then moving on from the cello to the stronger gypsy rhythm which formed the pervading theme of the dances.

When the work was completed they went wild, throwing flowers on to the stage, whistling and shouting with total lack of inhibition. Krista, who had been ready to clap her hands together, found instead that she was standing like the rest but that her fingers were pressed against her flushed cheeks and she was too excited to do more.

Later that same evening the first interval caught her unawares and she had difficulty forcing her way through the crowds who were making for the bar, so that she was late in reaching his dressing-room.

'I'm sorry.' She burst in through the door, annoyed to see that the fresh shirt she had put out so carefully had gone from the hanger.

'What?' He emerged from the tiny bathroom already changed into the fresh shirt, trying, with ill-concealed impatience, to fix the cuffs.

'Let me.' Without looking at him she went swiftly forward, frowning over the difficulty of sliding the cuff-links into the starched cuffs. 'There.' Her face was flushed when she raised it to his and her colour increased at the expression she thought she saw there.

'You were late.' Abruptly he turned away from her towards the glass where he began tying his tie.

Although there had been no hint of criticism in his manner Krista was at once on the defensive and busied herself with the black jacket he had tossed down over a chair. 'Yes, I'm sorry. I didn't realise the crowds would be so difficult to get through.'

'Here,' he seemed to have little interest in her excuse, 'can you do this?' His impatience was only too obvious. 'I don't know why we have to trouble with these darned things. It's the music that's important, not a lot of people dressed up as monkeys.'

Used to doing the same task for her uncle, Krista completed it without fuss, then held out the jacket so that he could slip his arms inside. 'You know, you don't really believe that.' She brushed his shoulders with one hand.

'What?' In the mirror he was studying her gravely. 'I don't believe we look like monkeys.'

'That as well.'

'What do you think I look like, then, Krista?' There was a faint challenging smile on his mouth as he swung to face her, the dark blue eyes had a strange glitter.

'What do you want me to say?' She raised her chin, refusing to let him know the effect he had on her. 'That you look very handsome? But you know that well enough already.'

'But that isn't the same, Krista, as hearing you say so.' He took her chin between two fingers, turning her face round to the light. She gazed back at him unflinchingly. 'And you, Krista, do you know how beautiful you look? That hazy violet shade finds a reflection in your eyes. Eyes,' his searched hers with an intensity that robbed her body of breath, 'eyes that I had thought were grey, but now I'm uncertain.'

Quite abruptly he let her go and turned away from her. 'What did you think of the music, Krista?'

'I thought it was sheer enchantment.' Feeling ridiculously weak, she leaned against the back of a chair. She wasn't even certain that her words referred to the music.

'Good.' He smiled at her briefly, brilliantly, then brushed past her towards the door. 'I hope you will enjoy the second part as much.' An instant later she was alone in the dressing-room.

Slowly she walked across the room and picked up the white shirt he had discarded, scarcely noticing that it was damp with perspiration while pushing it inside the bag of things she would have to take back to the hotel that night. Then with a shuddering little sigh she shook her hair back from her forehead and almost ran back to her seat in the auditorium.

After Budapest, there was Berlin, Salzburg, Rome. On without a break to Athens, Bucharest and back to Budapest for a final series of concerts before they had a short holiday in France. Krista was staggered by the sheer vitality of the man— that and the way that he seemed to lapse without difficulty into whichever language the people around him were speaking. Of course the main tongue was English and for that Krista was grateful, but whenever she had any difficulty Ludovic was able to come to her assistance.

Every day, it seemed, she learned something new about the man who employed her. She knew now that whenever he had completed a concert he went off alone for a long drive to help him to relax. It was something that had concerned her when she had first known about it, but her offer to chauffeur him had been laughingly dismissed.

'I doubt that you would be able to drive fast enough for me.'

'Aren't there any speed limits in this country?' They were in Greece at the time.

'I suppose.' He shrugged his wide shoulders and grinned at her. 'I never ask.'

'Don't be surprised if you see your name plastered all over the front pages, then!'

But he had gone off laughing at her, not knowing that she lay awake worrying about him until at last exhaustion overwhelmed her and she fell asleep. But always when she went down to the hotel dining room for breakfast she would find him there before her, all his attention directed to the reviews of the performance in the morning papers.

'Do they worry you?' she ventured to ask him

one day when he tossed them aside with a shrug, reaching immediately for the coffee pot and refilling his cup.

'I'm interested, but I can't pretend I'm worried by them. Most of them couldn't play God Save the Queen if you put them down at a piano, so why should I worry? If they say what I'm already thinking then perhaps I admit they might have something. Otherwise——' he smiled at her as he reached for a cigarette. 'Do you mind if I smoke?' Pointedly he waited for the assurance she gave.

'Although, what you would do if I said I did object to your smoking I don't know.' She looked at him severely as she poured coffee into her cup.

'Then I shouldn't smoke, *drágám*.' Smoke curled up so his eyes narrowed against it. 'I seem to remember that happened once before.'

'Yes. But then you were trying to coerce me.'

'Was I?' He raised his eyebrows. 'I didn't realise that.'

Krista laughed. 'Of course you were. You realised you were in a spot because Jerzy had to go home in a hurry and I was the first, probably the only person you could think of.' She knew she was fishing for compliments, but she didn't mind.

'Yes, you were the only person I could think of.' His admission was so straightforward that she gasped.

'Well, that's blunt enough!'

'You see, Krista, you're like all other women. There are times when you positively ask to be contradicted, and when one is too polite to do so, you're annoyed.'

'I'm not annoyed. Not in the least.'

'Come on! I can see it in the way your eyes smoulder. They're all smoky, like Etna erupting.'

'It's that cigarette you're smoking. Doesn't it

occur to you that you're ruining your health with those?'

'It does. But I shan't give up for that reason.' He lay back in his seat surveying her from a distance.

'Oh? And what would make you give up?' Cagily she eyed him.

'I can't think of anything.' He stubbed out the half-finished cigarette. 'When I want to I shall give up. In the meantime I enjoy it and shall continue. Now,' it was one of those abrupt changes in which he specialised and which Krista found so disconcerting, 'since you brought up the subject of Jerzy. You have checked all the arrangements for the trip to France. I know he had the flight tickets and had made arrangements for a car to be waiting for us at Paris.'

'Yes, I've seen to all that.' Krista's pride was slightly hurt that he had asked, because she had worked hard to make sure that all his travel plans had gone smoothly. At each airport a fast sporty car had been waiting for them, and the only snags had been caused by things over which they had no control. She reached for her document case and pulled out a folder. 'Do you want to check yourself?'

'No. But you are familiar with the engagements we have when we reach Brittany?'

'Perfectly.' Her voice was even colder. 'You're conducting a local orchestra in one of the churches.' Her eyes searched through the diary until she found what she wanted. 'At Trehaix. And we shall be staying with the Comte du Boulet just outside Loudéac.'

'With the Comtesse du Boulet. There is no Comte. She's a widow.'

'Oh?' She peered at the diary. 'I suppose it could be Comtesse. I thought it was Comte.'

'You'll like her enormously. She's one of my oldest friends.' Ludovic pushed back his chair and got up, reaching for his jacket which he had slung over the next seat. 'Now come on, I'll take you for a walk round town. Might as well make the most of it while we're here.'

Although she had spent some time wandering round the city on her own, Krista found the idea of going with Ludovic exciting, as the sudden shine in her eyes must have told him.

'Go up and put on something warm, *drágám*. The air coming from the river can be a bit chilly even at this time of the year.'

She needed no second telling, and while she was upstairs in her bedroom she hugged her pleasure to herself, excited even so early in the day by the warm and throbbing way he used the word *drágám* when he spoke to her. Of course now she knew that it was a term of mild endearment, one that he used with great frequency to his friends as well as to members of the orchestras. So long as they were female. And she had watched those others become warm and melting too. Once rather cynically she had wondered if he used it knowing full well the effect it had. But even that suspicion could not still the flow of warmth she experienced each time it was directed at her.

He was patient as they wandered along the Great Boulevard which circled the city, laughing with her as she pointed out a particular thing in a shop window which attracted her attention, telling her the names of many of the beautiful buildings they passed. They went into the Belvárosi Templom, one of Pest's most ancient churches, surprising the organist playing some Listz which they sat quietly enjoying for half an hour.

'Shall we go?' It was Ludovic who made the first

move, reaching out a hand for hers, smiling into her eyes when she turned to him. And it was a great comfort to her that he continued to link his fingers in hers while they tiptoed down the aisle until they reached the huge Gothic door on the south side, releasing her only to allow her to step ahead of him into the autumn sunshine.

When they had their fill of sightseeing and Krista admitted that her feet were aching, he put his hand on her elbow and summoning a taxi gave rapid directions to the driver before climbing into the rear seat beside her.

'Do you feel hungry?'

'Do I feel Hungary is what?' she teased, and laughed when he groaned. 'Yes, I do. I'm always starving by midday.'

'Good. Then I shall take you where you can have some of the best Hungarian food.'

A moment later they had been dropped at one of the many restaurants built out on to the river. Here they were welcomed aboard by the head waiter, speaking affably as if he knew the famous conductor, while he led them to one of the pleasantest tables directly overlooking the water.

Krista would scarcely have been human if she hadn't enjoyed the sidelong glances that her companion got wherever they went, and here on his native soil they were more frequent, less inhibited than anywhere. At the next table to theirs, two couples were sitting, and while the men pored over the menu, Krista saw how one of the women, a beautiful dark-eyed woman in her early thirties drew her friend's attention. She heard the murmured 'Hasek,' but a quick glance in the right direction showed that as usual he appeared not to have heard but instead was summoning the waiter who hurried over to offer the long menus with a

smile and to flick at the perfect white cloth with a
serviette.

'What would you like, Krista?'

'Some of that special Hungarian food you
promised me. I'll let you order.'

The upward flick of the long dark lashes, the
sudden brilliant look from those intensely blue
eyes made her heart flip over in her chest and she
was glad his eyes didn't linger to see the only too
familiar colour in her cheeks. With difficulty she
wrenched her eyes away from his figure, as
handsome and fascinating as ever in a light grey
suit with a darker rollneck sweater.

Beyond them, the river flowed swiftly, each
ripple catching the light from the sun, glittering as
blue and dark as his eyes. Another uneasy thought
struck her. What was it she had heard about the
Danube? It was only blue to those in love. But
surely . . . She drew in a sudden breath and put her
fingers to her mouth, raising her eyes to find
herself the subject of his quizzical study.

'You look concerned, *drágám*.' Just the word
had the effect of causing a shiver of emotion to
run through her. His eyes flicked from contemplation of her to nod at the waiter, who was pouring
golden wine into a glass. 'To you.' He raised the
glass in salute and drank. 'What caused the frown
on your pretty face?'

'Nothing.' Recklessly she took her glass and
gulped. 'Nothing, except that I didn't expect the
river to be that particular colour.'

'And what colour do you find it, Krista?' He
was watching her over the rim of his glass with
close attention.

The colour of your eyes, she thought.
Ridiculously. But with as much coolness as she
could muster she said, 'It's blue, of course. Just as

the song says.' She tried to still her absurdly racing pulses. 'What colour do you say?' Again she raised her glass to her lips.

'Like you, Krista.' Across the width of the table she could not be certain that his eyes were as teasing as his voice. 'I too think it's blue—a deep dark blue. But of course,' his look seemed briefly to caress, 'sitting at the window in the Kék Duna what other conclusion could we possibly reach?'

For a moment he lay back in his seat watching her bewildered expression, then he laughed, sat forward and reached across the table to cover one of her hands with his. 'This is the Kék Duna Restaurant. The Blue Danube.'

But Krista was scarcely able to take in what he was saying, for all her attention was concentrated on the trembling sensuous feelings which were quivering through her body. Feelings which the thoughtless stroking of his fingers against her wrist made almost unbearable. Painfully, recklessly she pulled her hand away from his disturbing touch to reach again for the almost empty wine glass. 'To the Blue Danube.' Her manner was flip, her voice just a shade strident for the time of day. Impossible to explain that that was her rather gauche means of defending herself from emotions she didn't understand. Yet she saw his face darken just a little and knew that in some equally incomprehensible way she had disappointed him.

CHAPTER THREE

SUMMER, which had been reluctant and fickle that year, seemed to have been saving herself for their journey through the Brittany countryside. It was early afternoon when they drove from Paris, passing small villages slumbering in the warm sunshine, the gold-coloured stone of the houses making a perfect background for the flowers that rioted in rampant confusion in gardens and along road verges.

Ludovic drove with the verve and dash which Krista had now become used to and which no longer caused her to press her feet down on to the deep pile carpets. It hadn't taken her long to realise that in this, as in most other things, he was more than competent, that it was safe for his passengers to relax in the knowledge that his liking for speed in no way was an indication that he was inclined to take risks.

They were driving through a sleepy village, Krista aware that her eyelids felt particularly, pleasantly heavy, that her head was beginning to nod, when quite unexpectedly she felt the car take a sharp turn to the right where she had expected it to go straight on.

'Ludovic?' Stifling a yawn, she pushed her spine back into the seat and sat up straight. 'Where are we going?' She turned to him.

'We are almost there now.' His brief glance, the white smile were precious but disturbing. 'I didn't want to wake you. The village we just passed through is Grimaud and the château is just about a mile further on.'

48

Almost as soon as he had stopped speaking they emerged from a leafy incline and ahead of them Krista caught a glimpse of elaborate, impressive stone gates. There they turned, going along a drive sheltered by tall poplars and leading to a clump of trees through which parts of the roof came and went teasingly. Krista sat forward in her seat, releasing her safety belt, anxious for her first sight of the house where they were to be guests of the Comtesse.

The trees which formed a protective girdle about the large house had the effect of increasing the dramatic impact on the visitors, for they came out of a dark tunnel where light seemed reluctant to penetrate to see it, elegant and glowing, bathed in the warm afternoon sunshine. The central front door, which was reached by a short flight of wide steps, was flanked by rows of identical windows each with a bowed metal windowbox from which geraniums in shades of pink and white cascaded. The windows on the two upper floors matched those on the ground but above the door were longer windows opening on to small balconies with elaborately wrought iron. Round the roof was a matching balustrade which with the flowers relieved a tendency towards severity.

'Here we are.'

Krista hardly heard Ludovic, she was so absorbed in studying all the details of the architecture, her eyes moving away from the house towards the gardens which descended on several levels to the right of the main building. She could just see some pink roses blooming in a burst of late colour, and farther away the sunlight reflected on a lily pond with the spray of water from a fountain disturbed by a faint breeze.

The sound of a door opening, a woman's voice

and the staccato noise of high heels on stone brought her attention back to the house, and she watched while a woman ran towards Ludovic, who having got out of the car was in the process of unlocking the boot. The driver's door was open, making it quite impossible to avoid hearing the conversation, although much of the rapid French was incomprehensible to her. But the tone of the voice was unmistakably affectionate.

Nothing could have stopped Krista's eyes searching in the rear mirror, and she saw the way Ludovic's arms closed about the woman, she knew even though that part was cut off by the line of the windows that the woman had her lips raised to his, that they were kissing. Abruptly she moved in her seat so that they were out of her vision, but she could do nothing about the excited conversation drifting in through the open door. The woman was young—that was the fact that struck her with the greatest force. She had come expecting the Comtesse to be elderly, or at least middle-aged, so it was a surprise, a shock to realise that she wasn't a great deal older than Krista herself.

She heard her own name dropped into the conversation and her heart gave an anticipatory flip. Then it was repeated, questioningly, lightly in the feminine voice and again in Ludovic's deeper tones.

'Oh, you'd best come and meet her.' He abandoned French for English at the same time as she heard them come round to the side of the car, knew that her door was being opened. 'I haven't had the chance to tell you that Jerzy had to go home unexpectedly and I shouldn't have been able to cope if Krista hadn't taken such pity on me.'

Krista found herself standing outside the car, a fixed smile on her face while she held out a hand towards the woman who still had Ludovic's arm casually draped about her. Without immediately understanding why, Krista was at once aware of being at a terrible disadvantage, but she managed to force out a few conventional words.

'How do you do, *madame*.' Then she looked into the woman's eyes and knew at once that her own appearance was at least as much of a shock, a very unwelcome shock at that.

'Barbe,' now it was Krista's turn to have the casual arm about her, 'this is Krista Ewing, who is just as efficient as Jerzy ever was. And Krista, this is the friend I've told you so much about, the Comtesse du Boulet.'

'But how indiscreet of you, *chéri*!' When the formalities had been completed and they were walking towards the house the Comtesse patted Ludovic reprovingly on the arm. 'Not to tell me about Miss Ewing before. There could have been the most awful *gaffe* if I had arranged for Jerzy to share a room with someone, as has happened sometimes. As it is . . .' She hesitated, appeared about to say something, frowned and changed her mind. 'But come inside. Henri will take up your cases presently. You must be longing for some tea.' She spoke English well and with a liquid accent which was entrancing, Krista decided regretfully.

They climbed the few steps into the wide elegant hall, their footsteps echoing across the huge gold and black slabs of marble. Ahead the staircase rose for a short distance from the centre before branching out to right and left to reach the upper floor. At the half-landing were huge marble urns, covers in gilded wrought iron that matched the balusters.

But as soon as Krista had time to notice these

things, and briefly to decide that although it was
very impressive it was hardly home-like, she and
Ludovic were swept into a large salon where at
one end in front of wide-open windows a low table
covered in white damask was laid for tea. Almost
at once an elderly maid came in carrying a heavy
silver tray which Ludovic at once relieved her of,
at the same time engaging the woman in a
laughing conversation which she seemed to enjoy.

Although she would have liked to freshen up
before having tea Krista found herself grasping a
cup and saucer of the finest china and shaking out
an immaculate napkin to protect the knee of her
blue denim jeans. Rather cynically she decided that
it pleased the Comtesse to put her at a
disadvantage, but as if able to read her guests's
thoughts the Comtesse offered an apology.

'Forgive me, *mademoiselle*, I should have asked
if you would prefer to be shown to your room
first.'

Krista, who had that instant taken a bite from
her sandwich, shook her head in denial, although
she could hardly hide from herself, and she
suspected her hostess, that her hands would have
benefited greatly from an interlude with some soap
and water.

'I was so excited at seeing Ludo again that it
drove all other thoughts from my mind. And he is
so very much at home here at the château that he
does not have to be asked such things.'

Krista risked a glance from beneath her lashes
at the dark man sitting opposite her, surprised
something almost like amusement on his face and
hastily transferred her attention to her hostess.
The Comtesse and Ludovic had embarked on a
discussion of the concerts he had promised to
conduct, and Krista had no compunction in

allowing the conversation to wash over her head while she studied the opposition.

In her own mind she had no hesitation in deciding the Comtesse represented exactly that. It had been apparent in the first shocked glance, in the sudden widening and the almost imperceptible narrowing of the black eyes, eyes that now were large and luminously beautiful as she laughed at something Ludovic had said.

Again Krista had the impression of being at a disadvantage, but now she understood only too clearly the reason for that first half-understood idea. The Comtesse was beautiful, but there was more to it than that. It would be impossible to deny that such a woman, petite with a dazzling dramatic beauty, would excite every protective instinct in a man, but as well she was elegant, with that unobtrusive style which sets the Frenchwoman apart. It was there in every gesture of her small manicured hands, the fingernails devoid of varnish but gleaming with years of careful buffing. It was in the set of her head, the glitter of the tiny diamonds in her well-shaped ears, in the plain beautiful way her black hair was knotted at the back of her head. And most of all it was in the citron yellow linen suit she wore, the shade making such a perfect foil for anyone of her colouring.

Krista could hardly subdue a feeling of yearning admiration. She judged the Comtesse to be about five years older than herself—and yet she seemed infinitely older in terms of life's experience and savoir faire than Krista could ever hope to achieve. Even if she lived to be eighty she would . . . With a start she realised that Ludovic was speaking to her, felt the hot colour run up in her cheeks.

'I was asking, *drágám*, if you would like to have

a rest. Barbe and I shall be going to town for the orchestral rehearsal, but unless you wish you need not trouble.' His mouth and his eyes smiled at her. 'You must be tried.'

'No, of course I'm not.' She put her cup down on to the table. 'But I would like to wash and change.' She stood up, pushing her blouse down inside her jeans. 'I feel quite grubby.'

'I should take it easy, if that is what you wish, *chérie*.' The Comtesse smiled as she got to her feet. 'And I can always act as your deputy if you wish.'

Krista was surprised by the feeling of obstinacy engendered by that smile. 'I shouldn't dream of imposing on you, Comtesse. Besides, I'm looking forward to seeing your wonderful cathedral. Ludovic has told me so much about it.' She followed her hostess to the door, along the corridor and up the stairs, walking ahead into the room when a door was held open for her.

'You think you will be comfortable!' From the Comtesse's manner it was clear the question was a mere formality.

'Of course I shall.' Krista forgot her irritation as she looked round the unexpectedly delightful room. 'It's a beautiful bedroom.'

'The bathroom is here.' A door in the row of fitted cupboards was opened, then the Comtesse walked across the room and looked out of the window at the view of the gardens. 'It's such a pity . . .' She hesitated in faint embarrassment which Krista felt was assumed. 'Men are so thoughtless. You understand these things, *mademoiselle*.'

'What things, Comtesse?' Krista felt cagily suspicious. 'Until I know what you mean then I can hardly understand.'

'Oh, it may not happen.' The Comtesse smiled insincerely, showing her perfect small teeth. 'It is simply that I shall be having the château full of guests for the concert, many of them staying overnight, and ...' she frowned, tapping one cheek with an impatient finger, 'I was depending on you being able to share with someone. If you had been Jerzy, I mean, of course. But let's not worry about that in the meantime—and please don't mention the matter to Ludo. I refuse to have him worried in any way before a concert.'

Krista, scarcely knowing what to say merely stared at the woman, understanding very well that her hostess meant her to realise clearly that her presence in the château was unwelcome. The silence between them lengthened until it became embarrassing and the girl forced herself to answer quietly.

'I quite understand, *madame*. You must tell me if you find you require my room for someone else. And of course I shan't speak of it to Ludovic.' She felt pleased when she saw the black eyes spark with sudden anger, but as if unwilling, ashamed even of her own feelings, the Comtesse turned away with a whirl of her pleated skirt.

'Then I shall leave you, *mademoiselle*. If you are sure you have everything you want. If not, then simply ring this bell.' She indicated a button beside the light switch.'Hortense will come up and give you what you need.' She paused with her hand on the door knob. 'We shall be leaving in half an hour—I hope that will be sufficient time for you to wash and change.' Her dark glance was an adverse comment on crumpled jeans and shirt.

'Quite enough.' No matter how much Krista resented the implication that she needed to do either, she forced herself to speak politely, but when the door closed behind her hostess she enjoyed a few moments of bubbling resentment. It wasn't a feeling with which she was familiar, nor one that she knew how to deal with, but for just a second she had the inclination to take one of the crystal ornaments from the dressing table and hurl it against the mirror, although almost at once she was able to smile wanly at such uncharacteristic reactions. Instead, she glanced at her watch and ran to the bathroom, pulling off her crumpled blouse as she did so.

It was taken for granted, by the Comtesse at least, that Krista should relinquish her seat beside the driver in her favour. And Ludovic too seemed to accept the change, although his touch on Krista's elbow might have been a tiny gesture of sympathy. If it was, she choose to ignore it and sat with her clipboard of blank paper on her knee as if to indicate that she was there only to work.

Above the hum of the engine she could hear little of the conversation in the front, but she told herself that she didn't want to be included in any event. It gave her the chance to study the Comtesse's hair-style, to admire and envy the casual perfection with which it was swathed at the back of her head and to notice that the neck and shoulders of her dark red silk dress fitted perfectly.

Ludovic too looked immaculate in his dark lounge suit and a shirt in a dashing shade of pink matching the rose he wore in his buttonhole. It was difficult to avoid the question of who had selected such a perfectly matched rose. She visualised Barbe—she thought the name was very aptly chosen, she visualised her going along the border of the rose garden, trying out the various shades until she found the one which suited perfectly. She imagined the deft fingers slipping it into the lapel, then perhaps she had lifted her face for his kiss of thanks.

'Krista! You haven't fallen asleep, have you, *drágám*?'

'Of course not.' Quickly she brought her thoughts back to the present, her eyes met Ludovic's in the mirror. 'I was admiring the countryside, that's all,' she lied.

'I was telling Barbe about our meal yesterday in the Kék Duna. I said we were arguing about the colour of the river.'

'And you thought it was blue, Krista? May I call you Krista?' The look she saw on the girl's face when she swung round in her seat must have signalled permission, for she smiled before she turned away again. 'You know what that means, Ludo *chéri*, it means that she is in love. They say that the Danube is only blue to those who love. I'm sure that back in Scotland she must have a lover whom she is pining to be with. It could hardly be otherwise with such a pretty girl,' Barbe declared magnanimously.

'In that case Ludovic must be in love too,' Krista countered sweetly. 'He too admitted it was blue.'

'Ludo!' Barbe's coy tones were nauseating, Krista decided, and she looked deliberately away from the pair in front, through the side window, although she was hardly aware of what she was seeing. But she heard Barbe's voice, low and teasing, continue, then almost at once was followed be a protesting laugh from Ludovic.

'Krista! I don't recall saying any such thing. I said we were sitting in the Kék Duna—I could hardly say anything else.'

'How like a man to say something and then almost immediately to deny he had said it!' Krista refused to catch his eye in the mirror, steadfastly looking out at the streets of the small town through which they were passing, relieved to find that her sharp tone had effectively killed the conversation yet perversely annoyed by the long-suffering glance she sensed from the driver.

Tréhaix had been built defensively on a hill with all the roads steeply inclining towards the large church which dominated the entire area. When they stopped in the square in front of the massive gates of the cathedral, gates which in olden times must have efficiently excluded invaders, Krista turned in genuine pleasure to the woman whom she had decided she disliked.

'How marvellous to have a church like this in such a small town!'

'Oui.' They climbed out of the car and stood looking up at the great façade. 'It is one of our most famous Renaissance churches and every four years we have a great summer festival of music. This year we have been fortunate enough to have a world-famous conductor. It took all my powers of persuasion.' She laid a slender hand on Ludovic's sleeve. 'Is that not so, *chéri?*'

'What?' He had been locking the doors of the car and seemed to have missed her last words. His smile encompassed both of his companions, but lingered perhaps a moment longer on Krista's face.

'I had to beg and plead, promise you ... the world in order to get you here for our festival.'

'Oh?' The wrinkling of his face implied doubt. 'Was I so very awkward? I hadn't realised. I thought that the main problem was my diary. Last year it was impossible to fit it in. This year, simply because Jerzy juggled my dates and postponed the trip to New York, I was able to accept.'

'Nevertheless,' Barbe pouted, 'I had to use all my wiles ...'

'You've had such a lot of practice,' Ludovic agreed amiably as they walked together towards the door.

Inside the huge building Krista stood for a moment looking up at the soaring arches before following the other two down the side aisle. It really was a perfect dress Barbe was wearing. That rich red shade suited her ideally and the high-heeled patent sandals were an exact match as well as drawing attention to her tiny feet.

She must have changed at top speed, for she had been waiting with Ludovic in the hall when Krista hurried breathlessly down the imposing staircase. Some demon had persuaded her to exert herself over her appearance, and she was pleased with the result. Her white lacy blouse with its high neck had a faintly Edwardian look, the full frothy sleeves reached to the elbows, their dazzling whiteness contrasting with the honey tan of her forearms. With it she wore a plain black skirt, yoked to show her slim waist, then flaring out to mid-calf length. Walking behind Ludovic and his companion, she could hear the whisper of the grosgrain silk against her legs and the tap of the impossibly high heels she had worn to give her one advantage over Barbe.

But in such surroundings it was impossible to dwell for more than a few moments on anything as fleeting and temporal as fashion—besides, the tantalising glimpses of the spotlit section of the church in front of the high altar was too obvious a reminder of the real purpose of their visit. They passed the last of the huge pillars obscuring their view, and at once a man who had been speaking to the members of the small orchestra assembled there turned and came forward to greet them.

Krista hung back a few moments while he and

Ludovic shook hands, laughed and spoke together rapidly in French. It was impossible for her to change her personality completely, no matter how she tried she could not throw off the lingering shyness which had been such a trouble to her all her life. She watched the Frenchman bend to kiss Barbe on each cheek with every show of affection, but all the time his eyes, dark and appraising, perhaps even a little admiring, were on Krista, noticing her faint blush with an amused raised eyebrow.

'Jean-Paul, this is Krista Ewing who has come from Edinburgh with me.'

'From Edinburgh?' He spoke with that liquid charming French accent so very much in keeping with his conscious Gallic charm, at the same time taking Krista's hand and raising it to his lips.

'And this, Krista,' now it was Ludo's turn to raise a comical eyebrow in her direction, 'is Jean-Paul Brissot, Barbe's brother. And I must warn you that he is the greatest flirt in France.'

'And the greatest trumpet player, *mademoiselle*.' In no way put out by Ludovic's description, Jean-Paul laughed. 'But tell me, what brings you here today? It is such an unexpected pleasure.'

'Krista has come to replace Jerzy.' Barbe's voice cut in on her brother's admiration for the newcomer. 'She is acting as Ludovic's secretary in the meantime.' There was no mistaking the hostility of the look she turned on Krista, although her voice was mild enough. And her voice, Krista realised, was all that mattered at the moment, for Ludovic had turned away towards the orchestra members so patiently awaiting his attention.

Krista took her seat quietly among the scattering of people who had come to hear the rehearsal for the following night's concert, surprised when Barbe dropped into the place beside her.

'Jean-Paul will astonish you, Krista. Although he plays at being the dilettante his music means everything to him.'

And when Jean-Paul, standing in front of the other players, raised his trumpet to his lips Krista understood exactly what Barbe meant, sympathised with her pride in her brother, for the notes that came from the instrument were sheer magic. It was the first time she had heard the Haydn concerto for the trumpet and orchestra, and she was dazzled as much by the brilliance of the playing as the beauty of the music.

Just then there was nothing of the playboy about him and the image which Krista had formed had to be dismissed, although looking at him in the intervals of his playing Krista understood exactly what Barbe meant when she spoke of him being a dilettante. To begin with, his dress, although immaculate, was a trifle unusual. Even at the height of Edinburgh's Festival absurdities she had never seen a man wear a lemon suit before. Only the fact that it was so expertly tailored and the obvious quality of the cloth redeemed it, but besides that Jean-Paul wore it with such an air that there was no inclination to think it more than daring yet somehow suitable for such a man. While the rest of the orchestra continued to play through the piece he occupied his rests in a quiet conversation, accompanied by extravagant gestures with someone on the left hand of the aisle. Once or twice Krista glanced with a shade of apprehension in Ludovic's direction, but the maestro continued to conduct without as much as a reproachful glance in the direction of the soloist. When they reached the end of the concerto there was a murmur of appreciation among the listeners, ignored by the musicians who were intent on hearing what Ludovic had to say to them.

Krista got up with a quick apology to Barbe and began to stroll round the church, feeling an unworthy edge of resentment that her hostess seemed to think it her duty to follow, offering explanations and translations of even the most elementary inscriptions, so that she sounded like a guide showing round a school party.

'You see here, this magnificent tapestry was worked after the plague of 1631 as a thanksgiving for the town's survival. And these tiles on the floor are older still. They were inspired by the knights who came back from the crusades and the Oriental designs they brought back with them. And naturally at Christmas this is where we have the crib and the Christ Child. I suppose you have the same in your own chruches.' The last comment was so innocent that Krista answered before she knew how leading it was.

'No, not so much. I'm not a Catholic and we don't go in so much for these things in the Church of Scotland.'

'Ah.' Barbe's look of satisfaction was almost immediately guarded. 'Tell me about yourself, Krista. How did you come to meet Ludovic?'

'As you might expect, through music. Last year he conducted for the Festival and my aunt met him then. This year they met again and became more friendly. Then when Jerzy had to leave in an emergency Ludovic asked me to take over for him.'

'Yes, I expect it was an emergency.' The black eyes surveyed Krista with no sign of warmth. 'How strange that he didn't even think to mention you to me when he telephoned, but . . .' Her voice trailed off.

With her cheeks suddenly warm Krista turned away, apparently absorbed in one of the many side chapels at the east end of the building. It was easy enough to add the words Barbe had been too polite to speak. 'I don't suppose he thought it was important enough.' That, she imagined, was the statement which had hovered on Barbe's lips, unspoken but implied. And the possibility that it might have a certain amount of truth made her eyes sting with tears.

Behind them she heard the orchestra begin to play some Vivaldi, and for once the music failed to soothe her agitation. Abruptly she walked away from Barbe, her heels tapping on the stone floor seeming to underline her disturbed emotions, which increased when she realised that her companion was not to be so easily dissuaded.

'Are you too a musician?' Barbe sounded genuinely interested.

'Me?' Krista asked inelegantly. 'No. I don't have any startling gifts, I'm afraid.' Turning quickly, she surprised a gleam in Barbe's eye. 'I do have an aunt who sings.' She couldn't have explained what made the foolish, slightly sardonic remark come to her lips.

'An aunt?' Barbe's eyes grew round and mocking. 'Really? One who sings.'

'Yes.' Krista had her back to one of the wide columns, giving her momentarily the impression of being at bay. 'It was from her that Ludovic borrowed me.'

For a moment the older woman stared, not quite understanding, then her laugh rang out, causing utter dejection in Krista. What on earth had possessed her to say that? Abruptly she pushed past the Comtesse, reaching the orchestra at the same time as the closing notes, hurriedly collecting her clipboard, making hasty little memos which she would type out later as reminders to Ludo.

It was something of a relief when at last it was time for them to return to the château, for Krista became weary of Barbe's persistently probing attitude. But the intimacy of the quartet who sat down to dinner in the family dining-room was something she found equally trying. In fact she suspected Jean-Paul had been instructed by his sister to pay as much flattering attention to their visitor as possible, a rôle which he seemed too willing to enjoy. And besides, thought Krista nastily, that left Ludovic free to give his undivided attention to the Comtesse. At any other time it might have been possible to tolerate being the focus of Jean-Paul's interest, but under the perceptive eyes of her employer, the indulgent approval of her hostess, Krista could only feel conspicuous and rather foolish. Barbe's stupid teasing warning to her brother about a young man in Scotland did nothing to soothe her feelings, and the gaze she turned on Ludovic was stormy and resentful.

'So, Krista,' Jean-Paul touched her wrist lightly, with every appearance of confidence in his own irresistible powers, 'I think I must exert myself to make you forget this young man you have left behind in Scotland. Is that possible, do you think?' The black eyes narrowed with conscious seductiveness.

Krista put down the empty coffee cup and pushed back her chair before answering. 'No,' her smile was saccharine-sweet, 'since there is no young man to forget, I don't think it is.' She got up, placing the crumpled white napkin on the table. 'Now if you'll excuse me, Comtesse, I think I shall go to bed.'

'So,' Barbe was not quite finished with her guest, 'no young man.' She sounded genuinely regretful. 'Then it is true perhaps what Krista told me, *chéri*.' Her soft white fingers were outlined against Ludovic's dark skin as she laid her hand over his. 'You merely borrowed her from her aunt.'

In the act of turning from the table, the girl paused, frightened suddenly by the moment's stillness about him, seeing with a shiver just how cold his expressive eyes could be. Deliberately his hand moved from under Barbe's and he reached for the cigar which had been smouldering in the ashtray.

'Krista said so?' Although his voice was mild, the flick of his eyes lashed her with anger, making her feel miserable with herself, bitter against him. And Barbe's laugh, light and condescending, made her want to lash out at them both. But instead she smiled, spoke with a derision that might have been for him but in fact was meant for herself.

'Borrowed like an old umbrella.' She repeated the words she had used before, then, her courage failing before his narrowed gaze, she turned and fled from the room.

CHAPTER FOUR

THE next few days passed in the crescendo of activity which always preceded a concert and with which Krista was becoming all too familiar. In this case she positively welcomed the work, because it helped her to forget the aching awareness caused by Ludovic's disapproval. Often in the weeks since she had left Edinburgh she, like many another, had had reason to quake when things went wrong, to shiver as he strode about the concert platform declaiming histrionically in that strange Magyar language. Once indeed he had picked up the baton which he seldom used at rehearsal, snapping it in a bout of frustration. But almost at once he had laughed at himself, raking his fingers through his long dark hair.

'Forgive me, ladies and gentlemen.' It was his softest sackcloth-and-ashes voice. 'Shall we try that passage again, please?' he asked gently, then proceeded to lead them through a faultless rendering of Beethoven's Choral Fantasia.

But this time was diffferent in that he kept himself under such tight control that only Krista herself was aware of any coolness between them. Once or twice she had noticed Barbe glance quickly from one to the other of them, trying to decide whether his formality might conceal some disfavour, but each time he seemed to turn his head deliberately from her. As if, thought Krista with passionate indignation, he doesn't want her to see that side of his nature. With me it doesn't matter. I'm just his dogsbody, to be shouted at

and pushed around and ... and borrowed. But
Barbe. . . she must be protected from the cold facts
of life. Her eyes glittered as she bent her head over
her notebook, hurrying with her rusty shorthand
as Ludovic issued a stream of imperatives at her.

Then gradually, as the excitement of the
preparation and rehearsals engulfed them, he
relaxed his disapproval. Possibly it simply became
too tiresome to maintain, but the formal manner
gave way almost imperceptibly to his normal
casual one, and Krista found that she was in great
danger of forgiving him.

Then on the very morning of the concert she
looked up from the breakfast tray which had as
usual been deposited on the small table by the
window to see Barbe opening the bedroom door
after a very gentle knock.

'Bonjour, chérie.' As usual Barbe was immacu-
lately perfect in a grey silk suit which at once made
Krista aware of her own deficiencies, although her
reflection had pleased her a few minutes before.

'Good morning.' She rose and rubbed one hand
down her pink jeans, aware that she ought not to
resent her hostess as much as she undoubtedly did.
'Will you sit down, Barbe?' She pulled forward
another small gilt chair. 'I'm just enjoying a
second cup of coffee. You have had yours?'

'Yes. Ludovic and I had ours a short time ago in
my room.' She paused and her dark eyes seemed
amused as they took in the younger girl's flaming
cheeks. 'Now he has gone to shower.' Elegantly
she lowered herself on to the chair, pausing for a
moment with a conscious attempt at diplomacy.
'There's a matter I must discuss with you, Krista.
An awkward matter.'

'Oh?' Scarcely knowing what to reply, Krista
stared back, and only then did she remember what

the Comtesse had said when she first arrived. 'You mean . . .'

'I am so sorry, Krista.' Barbe made a pretty helpless little gesture with her hands, shrugged her shoulders appealingly. 'I *do* regret this. If only Ludo had let me know in time then I could have altered my guest list, but as it is . . .'

'Nonsense!' Not for worlds would Krista have allowed Barbe any inkling of her feelings. Instead she slowly wiped her lips with her napkin and smiled. 'Of course I understand the situation. If only I can find accommodation in the *auberge* in the village I . . .'

'Ah, that's the point.' Barbe sounded really sorry. 'They have no rooms available, but I have found a room for you at the Cheval Blanc in Saint Christophe and . . .'

'Saint Christophe!' This time it was impossible for Krista to hide her dismay. 'But that's ten miles away!'

'Yes. But it was the best I could do. And I know that it is a very comfortable hotel, and I have persuaded the *patron* to give you his best room.'

'Thank you.' Krista made no attempt to hide her sardonic tone. 'I'm sure Ludovic won't mind taking me along.'

'Ah, but no,' the Comtesse interrupted with a wave of her hand. 'That is something else we must keep to ourselves, you and I.' She smiled as if she and Krista were confidantes. 'I shall have your things taken over during the morning. There's no need for Ludo to be troubled. In fact, I forbid you to mention the matter to him—I refuse to have him worried by domestic details just before the concert. This means a lot to me, Krista, and I am determined it will be the finest occasion in the history of Tréhaix and I shall allow nothing—

nothing,' she repeated with emphasis, 'to interfere with that.'

'You may rest assured, Comtesse,' Krista struggled to keep her voice even, 'that our wishes coincide in our determination to keep life as simple as possible for Ludovic. I merely thought,' with an appearance of innocent calm she turned to stir some cream into her coffee, 'that such an unimportant event would hardly be likely to disturb him in any way. But if you think otherwise,' the quick look in Barbe's direction surprised an expression of flashing anger, 'then of course we must keep it from him until the concert is over.'

But when Barbe had gone, turning and flouncing away with short angry steps, Krista found her own bravado was shortlived. For a long time she sat staring out over the garden, the delicious coffee growing cold in the cup she cradled between her hands, aware of nothing but the aching pain deep in her chest. It took her some time to identify the pain, still longer to associate it with the casual words Barbe had spoken when she had first come into her room. Or perhaps they had not been so casual. Of course they hadn't. Barbe was telling her quite deliberately the exact nature of her relationship with Ludovic.

The pain twisted again. It wasn't as if she didn't know what kind of man he was. Not that she had any direct proof, just the usual bits of gossip she had overheard in the weeks since she had come to join him. And she had been neither surprised nor shocked by what she had learned. It was almost inevitable that a man like him, handsome, gifted, travelling the world with the continuous aura of wealth and glamour about him, should have affairs. Indeed the wonder of it would have been if

he had *not* had that reputation. And she hadn't
minded, not really. Which made it all the more
confusing that now she did mind, painfully,
agonisingly, that he was having an affair with the
Comtesse.

The evening concert was the most exalting
experience of her life. Krista had no hesitation in
coming to that decision as she sat with the rest of
the audience and heard the closing notes of the
great concerto echo round the walls of the
cathedral, fade and die. Of course in that place
there was no applause, but when Ludovic turned
to them, smiled faintly through his exhaustion and
bowed, a sigh riffled through the tightly packed
rows. Her hands were clasped tightly together and
she watched as he held out a hand towards the
orchestra, towards Jean-Paul, then strode swiftly
towards the small ante-room behind the high altar.
    It was only after a few moments that Krista was
able to struggle through the crowds and join him
there, but even as she put her hand on the old-
fashioned iron lever she heard Barbe's voice,
speaking in French, congratulating him in the
most intimate affectionate manner.
    'I'm sorry, Ludovic.' She forced herself to go
inside, saw that already he had tossed aside his
formal coat and was rubbing his hair with a towel
while Barbe was sitting on the arm of a wooden
chair, smiling at him. 'I couldn't get through the
crowds.'
    'That's all right, *drágám*.' He grinned at her, at
once restoring completely their easy relationship
which Barbe had disrupted so deliberately, went
forward to a tiny mirror on the whitewashed wall
where he could see to restore his hair to some
order. 'What did you think?' He swung round,

surprising mutually antagonistic glances between
the two women. A tiny frown pulled the dark
brows together.

'I thought,' recalling the experience brought a
soft brilliance to her eyes, a glow to her cheeks and
her lips curved. 'I thought it was quite perfect.'

Her reply seemed to please him, for he turned to
adjust his tie. 'Yes, I too thought so. It was the
orchestra, of course. It is seldom that things come
together so perfectly for a performance, but this
evening it was so.' He reached for his coat. 'Now I
must get back and change. You are coming with
us, Krista?'

A warning look from Barbe reinforced the
words that had passed between the two women
earlier, and Krista shook her head. 'No, I want to
collect some things. I'll . . . come on later—as soon
as possible.' Not for the world would she have
given the other woman the satisfaction of knowing
how bitterly she felt her exclusion from the party
that was to be held at the château. Yet the last
thing she could tolerate would be to hear Ludovic
begging, or even demanding that his secretary
should be invited to the reception. Rather than
that she would endure a hundred solitary dinners
at the Cheval Blanc.

But that didn't prevent her, once she had
reached the privacy of the comfortable bedroom in
the hotel, of throwing herself on to the bed and
giving way to a few tears. But there were only a
few, because she knew very well that if she started
crying in earnest it might be hours before she
could stop again. And she wouldn't want to go
down to the dining-room with the signs of despair
written so clearly for anyone to see.

She got up and tidied her hair, frowning at her
reflection, trying to recapture the pleasure she had

felt in the pink and white outfit earlier, before
Barbe had assured her with absolute implacable
consideration that she need not trouble to return
to the château after the concert.

'You will be tired, Krista, and it will save
trouble later if you go straight to Saint
Christophe.'

As if that was the true reason! Krista
smoothed down the silky material, enjoying, in
spite of her low spirits, the way the pink jersey
clung to her narrow waist, then flared out about
her legs. The blouson top was cut rather loosely
on the bias, the diagonal stripes seeming to
emphasise the curves underneath. But now Krista
decided she could do without that, on such a
warm evening the camisole top on its own was
quite adequate for dinner in the small hotel. And
trying to put a brave face on things, she went
downstairs to the restaurant.

She had been sitting there for only a few
moments, studying the menu which the *patron* had
offered, when a young man stopped beside her,
hesitantly, with a *'pardon, mademoiselle.'*

It took Krista only seconds to recognise a friend
of Jean-Paul and Barbe, someone whose name she
had forgotten but who she knew she had met the
previous day during some of the rehearsals in the
cathedral.

'Monsieur . . .' Her expression was midway
between a smile and frown as she tried to dredge
his name from the recesses of her mind.

'Philippe Duclos.' He bowed slightly, the warm
dark eyes telling her more clearly than words how
much he admired her. 'You are alone, *mademoiselle*?'
The incredulity in his voice might have been
designed to flatter.

'Yes.' A faint colour stained her cheeks and she

busied herself with the menu again. 'Yes, Monsieur Duclos, I am alone.'

When he suggested that he join her for dinner Krista saw no reason to object, and she enjoyed his lighthearted conversation during the meal, finding it a welcome diversion from what would otherwise have been depressing thoughts.

'But what I can't understand, Krista,' Philippe was a very self-possessed young man and had at once swept aside any inclination towards formality, 'is why you should be here.' The fingers holding a cigarette in a short black holder made a sweeping gesture round the smart restaurant, 'instead of at the château.'

Now that she was on her third glass of wine Krista felt much less selfconscious about the reason for her exclusion from the party, 'Oh, it's quite simple really. There are so many people staying that there just wasn't room. I was quite happy to come here.' She could almost convince herself that it was so. 'Life has been so hectic recently that a little peace and quiet is more than welcome.' Then she thought of Ludovic and the smile faded from her lips.

'Mmm.' Philippe toyed with his coffee cup. 'You are sure that the reason is not more emotional, more feminine than the one you are suggesting?' He spoke English well with a strong but attractive accent.

'More feminine?' She didn't quite understand how his mind was working. 'What can you mean?'

'Can't you imagine,' he leaned forward and put his hand over hers as it lay on the pink linen cloth, 'that perhaps dear Barbe is just a little jealous that the maestro has found himself a pretty young secretary? You are quite different from Jerzy, n'est-ce pas? You have seen him?'

'Jerzy? No.' Krista shook her head slowly. 'Ludovic hoped that he might be able to come to Budapest one night, but it seems his father is still very ill and it was impossible for him to leave the family business. But why,' she returned to his theory, 'why should Barbe be jealous of me?'

'You must know that yourself without me telling you. But what I can say is that she has been trying for the last few years to bring Ludovic to heel. She is a very rich woman, of course. Her husband was many years older than she and since he died four years ago she has spent much time going round the world, indulging her passion for music. And I think it would suit her very well to be married to one of the world's leading conductors. Besides which,' the light voice was full of amusement, 'he is a man who will always be attractive to women. Don't you agree?'

Krista coloured, became conscious of his fingers tightening round hers and tried unsuccessfully to pull them away. 'I suppose so.' She tried to give the impression that she hadn't until that moment given the matter a great deal of attention, then with a great effort diverted the conversation from that particular line. 'You seem to know a great deal about their lives. How is that?'

'Oh,' he smiled, his handsome, slightly weak features sparkling with amusement, 'I have been friendly with Jean-Paul for many years, since we met the first day we went to school. From him I learn much of what happens at the château, so I know how Barbe's mind works.'

'Perhaps——' Krista's attempt to withdraw her hand was successful this time, 'perhaps you ought not to be telling me this. I'm sure Jean-Paul only discusses these matters in confidence.'

'Peut-être,' he shrugged, but showed no sign of

taking her words seriously, 'but I doubt it. Jean-Paul and his sister maintain a certain appearance of cordiality, but deep down they are not friendly. He did not approve of her marrying simply for money and position. Her husband was not ... respected, you understand.'

'I see,' said Krista, who didn't—not really. But nothing that she had learned gave her any encouragement. All the cards seemed to be in Barbe's hand. She had looks, apparently unlimited money, position, which when added to her undoubted interest and knowledge in music would seem to offer every advantage. 'But how,' in spite of herself she could not pretend a lack of interest, 'is it that *you* are not at the château this evening? I would have thought that as you're such a friend of Jean-Paul and as you're on the committee which arranged the concert you would have been one of the guests.'

'Oh ...' for a moment he looked embarrassed then he smiled at her, 'perhaps they simply forgot to send my invitation. Not every member of the commitee was asked. Anyway——' he leaned forward again, reaching for her hand, raising his eyebrows in rueful resignation when moving swiftly she linked it with the other in her lap. 'Anyway, I am pleased that I am here rather than there.' A flicker of a shadow across his face belied that remark. 'Otherwise I should not have had the pleasure of being with you. Now tell me, may I see you tomorrow evening?'

But Krista, although she had found the evening more tolerable with him than it would have been on her own, had no inclination to advance their acquaintance and made the excuse that her work prevented her from making any plans for the next few days, an excuse that Philippe accepted with some reluctance, giving a philosophical shrug and a smile of defeat only when she pushed back her chair with some finality.

It was the shrilling of the telephone close to her ear that brought her next morning from a sound dreamless sleep. For a long moment she lay snuggling deeply under the duvet, trying to ignore the clamour which threatened to drag her from her warm comfortable oblivion, but at last she stretched out a hand and pulled the instrument close to her ear.

'Krista.' It was Ludovic's voice, brisk, confident and yet giving the distinct impression that he wasn't too pleased with her.

'Oh, Ludovic,' She yawned noisily, 'you woke me. What time is it?' Her eyes struggled to focus on her watch.

'Krista—you are alone?'

It was an instant before the audacity of the question penetrated her mind and she answered indignantly, 'Of course I'm alone! I just said, didn't I, that you woke me.'

'Hmm.' His manner relaxed a little. 'The one does not always follow the other, *drágám*.' Then briskly, before she had the chance to make any further protest, he went on, 'I have a great urge, Krista, to get out into the country for the day. Last night I was deprived of the opportunity to drive like a bat out of hell round the neighbourhood, so today I must. You will come with me.'

Krista's fingers shook slightly as she pushed the hair back from her face. 'Into the country?' It seemed to her that they were already in the country, but apparently he saw nothing peculiar about his suggestion.

'Yes. I thought we could go swimming, so bring your bikini, Krista. Oh, and anything else you might need, because I intend to make a day of it. See you in half an hour.' He replaced the receiver before she had any opportunity of commenting.

Nothing, nothing, she decided, could be quite as wonderful, quite as unexpected as this. Even the realisation that it was still only seven-thirty could not diminish her anticipation. She threw back the bedclothes and ran across to the wardrobe, trying to decide what would be suitable for 'making a day of it'.

In the end she opted for something fairly simple, and when she saw Ludovic get out of the car and come striding across to the main entrance she was glad she had abandoned her early inclinations for semi-smart outfits. He was in black linen slacks with a pink shirt open at the neck and showing a disturbing amount of dark chest. Knotted by the sleeves about his neck was a black cashmere sweater, one he had bought when they were in Rome and which she knew had been hideously expensive.

The dark blue eyes looked approvingly at her sand-coloured safari suit and he held out a hand for the large raffia bag which held all her bits and pieces. 'Ready?' One dark eyebrow arched questioningly and he seemed to take her smile for assent.

It was pleasant in the early morning sun to drive in an open car, and Krista was surprised to find herself consciously relaxing as the wind caught at her hair, tangling the deep gold tresses until she reached into the bag for a silk kerchief which she tied round her head. Then she sighed in pleasure, sank deeper into the leather seat and pulled her sunglasses from her pocket.

'You have breakfasted?' Ludovic shot a glance in her direction.

'No. But it doesn't matter.' She was determined
that nothing should break the perfect calm which
existed between them at this moment.

'Of course it matters.' He lookd at the heavy
gold watch on his wrist. 'I know a place where we
can stop and have coffee and fresh croissants,
would that suit you?'

'Lovely!' Her head turned for a moment in his
direction, so she could enjoy the firm lines of his
profile, taking pleasure in the way the long silky
hair was riffled by the wind. She had a longing to
put a hand up to his cheek, dreamed for a moment
of him catching her fingers, holding them tenderly
close to him as if he were anxious to prolong the
sweetness of their contact. Her mind was drifting
towards still more tantalising absurdities when he
swung the car off the road and into the courtyard
of an hotel.

They were sitting facing each other as they had
done so often since leaving Edinburgh and he was
watching her pour coffee, much as he always did
when his attack came. And it was so sudden, so
unexpected that the hand pouring cream into the
dark brew jerked, spilling some into the saucer of
her cup.

'Tell me, Krista,' his voice had an accusing edge
which she disliked, 'tell me why you ran out on me
last night.' He stirred the scalding liquid, then
raised the cup to his lips without taking his
probing eyes from hers.

'Ran out on you?' His challenge was so
unexpected that for a moment she could hardly
think, she merely stared back at him, her grey eyes
wide and startled.

'You know what I mean.' He ignored the basket
of rolls which she offered. 'Who gave you
permission to go off without as much as asking me

if it was in order? Was it so important for you to keep your rendezvous?'

'Rendezvous?' His effrontery made her gasp.

'I wish you could break yourself of that habit,' he said irritably, 'repeating everything I say. It is most trying.'

The unfairness of this brought an angry reply to Krista's lips and her eyes flashed her own irritation. 'Remind me some time to tell you about *your* bad habits!' Then she held her breath, wishing she had hung on to her original intention to pursue a calm happy day.

As if to confirm her fears she watched the dark eyebrows come together in an angry frown, the always dark eyes grow still darker while Ludovic contemplated her with distaste. Then slowly, reluctantly his displeasure faded, the eyebrows resumed their normal line and the mouth hinted at a smile.

'So, Krista,' he spoke slowly and with a disturbing sibilance, 'you *do* have a temper. Beneath that oh, so calm exterior, something more exciting smoulders.'

'Not at all.' In an attempt to put things back to where they had been she disguised her feelings and reached out to take one of the croissants, spread a corner liberally with butter and cherry conserve and popped it into her mouth. Only then, when she had completed the ordinary little task, did she feel safe to raise her eyes again to his. 'I *am* calm. There are no hidden exciting fires smouldering deep down inside,' at least, privately she qualified that statement, I hope there aren't, 'only I don't see any particular virtue in being a complete doormat.' The calm with which she faced him was entirely assumed. 'No matter how much you would prefer it.'

'I see.' His voice was aggravatingly full of deep-down amusement and he pretended he was viewing their relationship from an entirely new angle. 'It is a shock to find this out after so long, *drágám*.' As always that word caused an uncontrollable surge of emotion deep inside her. 'So I find that the very reason for choosing you as my P.A. is nothing but an illusion.'

Krista, well aware that she was being teased, struggled with the inclination to giggle. 'If you imagined I was going to be a doormat, then yes, I'm afraid it was.'

His laugh, the way he threw back his head showing the long dark throat, made her heart flip and she could no longer control the smile that showed her response.

'So, Krista——' he seemed to have changed his mind about the croissant and she watched the long dark fingers wield the knife to split one, saw the white teeth bite into the pastry, 'you disappoint me.' But his eyes contradicted the words.

'I'm sorry,' she said meekly.

'No, I am. Sorry for trying to browbeat you. It was perhaps my disappointment at finding you did not wish to come to the reception. I wanted to share the whole evening with you.' The blue eyes seemed to be seeing her for the first time. 'But you are so young, and I must show more understanding. Barbe told me so, and she must be right.'

'Barbe . . .' again she was busy with coffee pot and cream, 'told you . . . what?'

'Why, that you had a young man. That he had invited you out to dinner.'

Krista, in spite of the way her heart was hammering, tried to subdue the urge to burst out with the complete story. After all, suppose he was in love with Barbe—her heart twisted, suppose he

meant to marry her, then it would be impossible to
let him know exactly what had happened. 'I'm
afraid Barbe made a mistake.' She smiled across
the table at him. 'It was simply that when I knew
how difficult it was for her to fit in all her guests, I
. . . suggested it would be easier to move to the
hotel.'

She watched the frown return to his face as if he
were trying to recall exactly what had been said to
him the previous evening, then his face cleared and
he smiled. 'So,' he sighed, 'then I must have made
a mistake. Some misunderstanding . . . Forgive
me, *drágám*. And all evening I was worrying
about you, wondering who this man might be.
And all the time you were alone.'

'Well . . .' Krista began, then stopped. Perhaps it
was better to leave things as they were. Additional
explanations would only confuse things further,
and besides, there was something about her
meeting with Philippe Duclos which she didn't yet
understand. An elusive feeling that she might have
been set up. And yet why . . .?

'Shall we go now, Krista?' Ludovic was restored
to his most charming, and not for the world would
she have said anything to provoke him again.

They stopped to do some shopping in a tiny town,
wandering among stalls laden with a bewildering
selection of foodstuffs and eventually buying some
rolls and pâté, a tiny piece of local cheese and a
bag full of ripe peaches which together with a
bottle of wine would make their lunch. Then they
drove further, seeming to Krista's now utterly
confused sense of direction always to be leaving a
major road for a minor, until at last they were
creeping along a rutted path, little more than a
cart track, to their left fields rich with golden

wheat, to the right a canopy of blue sky and
beneath them, the rolling breakers of the Atlantic
Ocean.

'How on earth did you find this place?' When
she had changed into her swimming things in the
privacy of the car and run across the few yards of
white sand to where he had thrown down a rug,
Krista sank down on her knees, averting her eyes
from that dark powerful body now dressed in
figure-hugging black trunks.

'Oh,' he spared her a quick glance, probably
ascribing to shyness her refusal to part with the
jacket which matched her bikini, 'we've come here
many times in the past. It has always been a
favourite, it is so peaceful.'

And no need to ask who 'we' were, thought the
girl with a stab of emotion. Who else could it be
but Barbe?

But even that thought could not depress her for
long. Not on such a day and in such a spot.
Behind them rose low cliffs giving total protection
from any breeze which might spring up and
transforming the small bay into a total suntrap.
There was scope for many kinds of beach activity,
rocks and tiny pools for pottering, not too
boisterous waves for swimmers and masses of
warm sand for simply lying on—and that was
what she intended doing, she informed Ludovic.
To underline her commitment, she lay back on the
rug, pulled her dark glasses from the top of her
head and closed her eyes.

'Later.' At once the sun-specs were removed and
his torso intervened between her and the sky when
her eyes flew open in protest. 'Later, Krista.' His
voice had that caressing quality which she adored
and distrusted. And she was right to distrust, she
thought as she became conscious of her heartbeats

hammering in her ears, of his naked chest leaning even closer to her in a blatant challenge. 'You may sleep later, but now ...' he might have been suggesting they make love first, her agitation was so profound, '... now I suggest that we should swim.' For a long time he looked down at her, his eyes reflecting some of her own uncertainty, before he dropped the sunglasses back into position.

He got to his feet with one powerful yet easy motion, held a hand out to clasp hers and pulled her to her feet. For a moment they stood facing each other, Krista swore she could feel the warmth of his body, then almost laughed at her wild imagination.

'Come on, then,' with a gesture that suggested principles abandoned she pulled off the sleeveless cotton jacket and threw it down on the rug, but the expression on his face robbed her at once of her resolve, made her even more aware of the situation they were in. Alone, miles from anywhere, with only a few strands of cotton between them and ... Her mind veered away from such distracting ideas.

'Come on, then!' Suddenly Ludovic was his normal mercurial self and the hand reaching out for hers was as dispassionate as a brother's, pulling her down to where the sea was foaming over the hot dry sand. Krista gasped as the cold water closed over her head, laughed up into Ludovic's face as she surfaced. There was no doubt about it, all those old stories about cold showers being effective for certain conditions had a great deal of truth! Only—she struck out from the shore away from him—possibly they would be even more effective if the source of the problem could be removed.

'For the time being I shall allow you to do that,

Krista.' They were back on the beach and she had
stretched out again on the rug. 'But not for long, I
promise.' But she didn't dare to open her eyes
when she felt him stretch out close to her, so close
that she would have sworn she felt the warmth
from his body. She reached out a hand for her
cover-up.

It was the clink of glasses that woke her and
when she sat up she saw that Ludovic had
arranged their purchases on paper bags on the rug
and that he was pulling the cork from their bottle
of white wine.

'Oh,' she stretched luxuriously, 'I had a lovely
sleep!'

'I noticed.' But there was no teasing in his voice,
only a kind of indulgent tenderness which was
echoed in the way his eyes lingered on hers.

'Do you always carry a bottle opener?' It was to
cover her real feelings that she asked the question.
Anything to distract that intent gaze which was
making her tremble.

'Always,' he grinned. 'And the glasses and
knives are by permission—no, I mean they are *not*
by permission of the Château d'Aubrac.'

'I see.' She sipped from the glass he held out to
her. 'I suppose even now they could be counting
the crockery.'

'Perhaps.' He lay back on the sand, smiling and
watching her through narrowed eyes. Then,
unexpectedly. 'Why don't you take off your jacket,
Krista?'

'All right.' Determined not to allow her cheeks
to flame, she put down her glass and shrugged her
arms out of the cotton blouse, then watched as he
pulled it towards him across the sand, rolled it into
a ball and used it for a pillow—all without taking
his eyes from her.

'You have a very pretty figure, Krista. You
ought not to go to such lengths to hide it.'

'I don't!' she protested, and taking up the glass
gulped at her wine.

'You do,' he teased. 'You know you do.'

'Well,' she said huffily as she stared out at
something of absorbing interest on the far
horizon,'if I'd known you wanted me to go about in
a bikini most of the time I would . . .' She faltered.

'You would what, *drágám*?'

'I would have told you to . . .' the absurdity of the
conversation struck her, 'to go to the devil!'
Laughter bubbled from her and she lay back
helplessly on the sand.

'Be careful.' He was leaning over her, his eyes
sharing the joke with her while his fingers
disengaged hers from the glass. 'Be careful of the
château crystal.'

Abruptly, suddenly tortured by the nearness of
him, Krista felt all her amusement swept away,
and at the same time the smile faded gradually
from his face, his eyes grew serious.

Aware that her heart was hammering, she put
up a concealing hand, encountered the silky skin,
the crisp curling hair of his chest. Then Ludovic's
mouth was on hers, warm and sweet, utterly,
inexplicably distracting.

'Krista.' When the kiss had ended she tried to
wrench herself back from the enchanting dream
world she had visited, saw his eyes dark, disturbed
above her as he spoke her name again. 'Krista.' His
fingers curled a strand of her hair and he looked at it
thoughtfully for a moment before he grinned.

'That's what it's for, after all, *kedvesem*. Kissing
is for pleasure.' And briefly, casually he dropped a
kiss on the tip of her nose, the kind of kiss that
brought her no pleasure at all.

CHAPTER FIVE

AFTER they had eaten, they drifted along the shore, looking in pools, picking up one or two shells, trying to catch in cupped hands some of the tiny creatures which inhabited the busy world just beneath the sea's surface. And all the time Krista was very careful to keep a certain distance between Ludovic and herself. She felt that she would scream if he were to drape an arm round her shoulder, to smile down at her in a friendly, affectionate way. Not when every nerve of her body was yearning, almost demanding a repeat performance of his kiss.

And to give him credit, he showed no sign of wanting to undermine her self-control. In fact he too might have been trying to keep his distance. Probably he had been able to sense something from her reaction, realised that his casual caress might be misinterpreted by the inexperienced girl he knew her to be. The thought was so stinging that in an effort to prove herself otherwise she turned on him with a dazzling, sophisticated smile. But the brilliant quip with which she had been about to reinforce her defences died on her lips when she found him looking at her, his eyes not quite concealed behind his sunglasses had a faintly, not puzzled exactly, but ... wondering.

As abruptly as she had looked up she returned her attention to the pool over which they were crouched. She put her fingers into the water, saw the surface and their images shiver with the disturbance. When it grew still again he was walking away from her.

'Come on, Krista.' From the edge of the water he turned to speak, his face restored to its habitual off-duty calm. 'Time for another swim.' And without waiting for her reply he waded out into the surging waves. And even though she still found the water cold she knew that his suggestion had everything to recommend it.

By the time they climbed out of the water and back up the shelving beach Krista was able to laugh at her stupid reactions. It was all a case of too much involvement with one man, allowing her natural sense of perspective to be distorted. Not that it was to be wondered at, she assured herself with a shade of compassion for the silly creature whose existence she had just nipped in the bud. The situation had simply gone to her head. All the adulation for the maestro had begun to rub off on her. So that when Barbe had made her a perfectly understandable suggestion, she had allowed herself to be all hurt and moody.

But now she could look at the stretched-out body of the man beside her on the sand and feel not a twinge. She jumped as his eyes flicked open and saw her standing there studying him, then she went on rubbing the nape of her neck, a blink and a yawn averting her gaze to a rock a few inches from his head. But before she could remark on the imaginary crab which had just scuttled from sight he sat up, linking his arms about his knees and sighing.

'It's been a lovely day, Krista.'

The approval in the lazy sensual tones in his voice brought the quivering back to her stomach and she sank on to the rug beside him. 'Yes.'

'Let's prolong it, shall we?' He turned to look at

her, frowning just a little, his fingers crumbling some dried sea plant which was littered along the beach. 'Can you bear to?'

'Of course.' It was a breathless little statement.

'You do not feel you have to go back? To do your hair or something like that?' His eyes moved from her mouth to the curls drying on her shoulders.

'Are you trying to tell me my hair looks a mess?' Without waiting for an answer she reached towards her handbag for her comb.

'Of course not,' he said coolly. 'It doesn't.' But when he said no more Krista was overwhelmed with a sense of disappointment and anti-climax.

'I think I'll go and change.' She got up, collected her things and walked towards the car, which was parked higher up, on the path that wound down almost to the beach. And all the time she longed to turn round, to find out if Ludovic was looking at her with that same taut expression. But she forced herself to walk on calmly, not hurrying, until when she reached the path a change of direction made it natural for her to glance back towards where she had left him. Then it was to find that far from watching her, he had gone back into the sea and was swimming across the bay with his steady powerful crawl.

The bikini she discarded was a little more than the two tiny scraps of material usually described by the word, and she wondered if she ought to have been more daring in her choice. But what had seemed perfectly appropriate for the cruise with Lady James last year was perhaps a bit conservative for Brittany, where she had heard that nude bathing was more the rule than the exception. Anyway, she still liked the hot red and black zig-zag pattern, and perhaps the three minute triangles were more for girls without busts than those with.

In her roomy bag she had brought a camisole
top in a stretchy jersey, the deep bronze colour
making a sophisticated contrast with her pale suit,
and when she had brushed back her hair she was
able to conceal its unruly curls in an almost
matching scarf. She took a bit of trouble with her
make-up, considering she had plenty of time as
Ludovic was in no mood to abandon his leisurely
swim so she was free to experiment.

. There were one or two false starts, the aubergine
eye-shadow which looked so effective on Barbe was
a mistake, and Krista regretted wasting so much
money trying to copy the style. In the end she was
pleased with the smear of brown eyeliner which
seemed to complement both her suntan and the
apricot gloss she wore on her lips. A few moments
with the mascara brush made her naturally long
dark lashes an even more effective fringe than
usual, and a little practice over the last few days
had done much to diminish her habit of poking
herself in the eye with the brush.

All in all, she was pleased with herself when she
snapped shut her compact and stowed her make-
up case back in her handbag just as Ludovic, fully
dressed, came up the path. His eyes swept over
her, causing confusion so that she leaned inside the
car pretending to be occupied tidying the interior,
grateful that he had made no silly remarks about
her appearance.

For the next hour or so their journey about the
countryside had a rather aimless quality, as if they
were both so preoccupied that neither had any
time to consider where they were going. But at last
Ludovic mentioned tea, and Krista gratefully
realised that she could drink a gallon of the stuff. In
the end she was satisfied with a large pot, shared
some delicious pastries, and by the time they left

the café and returned to the car they were both
restored to their normal humour.

Then Ludovic, deciding that it was time she
learned something more about the history of the
area, took her round several village churches,
assuming the role of guide as he thumbed his way
through the Michelin he had found in the car. It
was a mood Krista had never seen before, gentle,
self-mocking, droll, one she enjoyed so much that
she exerted herself to become the foil, the culture-
hungry foreign tourist.

It was growing dark when they drove into the
town of Massian and the restaurant which
apparently Ludovic had remembered and had
always hoped to revisit. Already the place was
fairly full, but they were fortunate to be given a
tiny round table for two, tucked away in a corner
with a view over the harbour where the lights of
fishing boats were constantly coming and going.

'Now,' he smiled at her in the subdued lighting,
'unless the management has changed I can promise
you a superb meal.'

And afterwards Krista always believed it had
been, although she was never certain that her
reaction was solely concerned with the food. She
had a vague recollection of some kind of lobster in
a rich creamy sauce, then duckling with a crisp
sweet skin which they ate with salad, cheeses
which she refused and finally a dish of wild
strawberries which were irresistible.

When she was stirring the strong black coffee
which she hoped would restore her to some kind
of sensibility she looked up to find his eyes, as they
had been so frequently during the meal, on her. He
lay back in his chair, even more forceful than
usual with the dark rolltop of his sweater seeming
to add something to his style.

So often at rehearsals she had seen him like this, simply dressed in jeans and polo sweater. But then his hair was often unruly, a result of the many times he had thrust an exasperated hand through it. Now it was brushed back with just one silky lock falling down across his forehead.

'You enjoyed the dinner, Krista?'

'Of course—it was delicious. But I'm afraid I've eaten too much. I can hardly move.'

'For that I have a plan,' he said somewhat mysteriously, but before she could ask what, he picked up the glass and studied the remains of his wine through narrowed eyes. 'And the wine too was pleasant, *n'est-ce pas?*'

'Yes.' Krista, who might have been drinking the cheapest supermarket plonk for all the difference it made to her, raised her glass and frowned at it with discernment. 'Yes, the wine too was perfect.' She drank rather injudiciously. 'Everything was perfect.' And she hiccupped.

'You would like a liqueur?' Ludovic raised a challenging eyebrow and grinned when she shook her head. 'I wasn't going to allow you to have one, in any case.' One casual raised hand brought the waiter. 'But I'll allow myself one.' He looked deep into her eyes. 'As it's a special occasion.'

'A special occasion,' she prompted when the waiter had gone to fetch the cognac.

'Yes. I always consider it a special occasion when I have completed one programme of engagements.' His smile told her he knew she had been expecting some more intimate reference, but she was too happy to be embarrassed by the thought. 'Now we have a few weeks before we begin the next programme, is it not so? And you realise, Krista, that will take us back to Edinburgh. Back home for you, *drágám.*'

It was as well that the waiter reappeared with the cognac and that he bustled about for a few moments, clearing away the coffee cups, flicking the tablecloth with a large white napkin. If it had not been for that diversion, Ludovic might have noticed the stricken look on the girl's face as she wondered if that meant the end of her association with him. After all, it had only been for a few months. Perhaps he was trying to remind her, very gently, of that unappealing fact.

But that was not a thought which could dismay her for long, especially when Ludovic forced her out into the soft warm night, insisting that a walk along the harbour would do them both a great deal of good.

'I'm too tired, Ludovic.' She yawned but gave in happily enough when he pulled her hand through his arm.

'You can't be tired. We've done nothing all day but lie on the beach. Remember all that sleeping you did this morning? How can you be tired?'

'I don't know, but I am. I suppose it's all that wine.'

'You'll be telling me next that you're not used to it.' There was a faint comforting pressure from his arm.

'You wouldn't believe me.'

'I would.' Tonight he was all indulgence. 'But I don't believe you are tired. You mustn't be tired. For I told you, I have a plan to help you get rid of all those calories you ate at dinner.'

'Don't remind me!' she complained. 'I'll be putting on pounds if I stay in France much longer!'

'That's another reason why you need some exercise.' And as he spoke he led her away from the quayside, up one of the many narrow streets meandering through the old part of the town.

'We came down this way when we came in, didn't we?'

'We did. And that reminded me of something I had forgotten—oh, it must be five or six years ago, we came disco dancing.'

'We?' The moment she asked the question she felt she could have bitten her tongue but he answered easily enough.

'Barbe and I. And one or two others.'

'Oh . . .' The 'one or two others' served to ease the constriction in her chest and she was able to smile up at him as he turned her round to face him.

'Shall we go, Krista?' While he waited for an answer the beat of distant music drifted towards them, a throbbing sensuous sound which seemed to fill her with a daredevil abandon. At the back of her mind was the thought that she *must* score against Barbe. But at the front of her mind was the simple urge to obey her instincts.

'Yes, let's go.' How could she say anything else when Ludovic had both hands on her shoulders, when he was looking down at her with that light enquiring expression? In spite of herself her breathing quickened, her pulses seemed to race in time to the music.

When they reached the source of the noise the deafening beat reached up from the cellar, filling the surrounding square with a vitality which was inescapable. Ludovic took her hand while they ran downstairs, paid the woman sitting behind the glass in the little box office and led Krista forward to join the others who were already twisting and gyrating to the music.

It was exciting to take part in this joint

experience with so many other people, some young, others not so young, many of whom she suspected were holidaymakers from the several large camping sites she had noticed on their travels about the area.

About them she could hear snatches of German, English, Dutch, even a little French as well as other tongues more difficult to identify, but it was all good-humoured, happy, a great relaxation at the end of a day which had been for most of them controlled by sun, sand and sea.

The main room of the cellar was large, darkly painted, so the effect of flashing lights, sudden brilliant explosions of colour were all the more effective. All that, the weird sensuous music which at any other time she would have considered an assault, the couples gyrating wildly, intensely, but most of all the man opposite her, were combining to bring her excitement to a fever pitch. It was all so unexpected, finding herself in this situation with him, something she could never have imagined. For surely this kind of music and the great Hasek did not go together.

And yet they did. Indisputably they did. With every sinuous move of his body, with each careless snap of his fingers he demonstrated it. He moved in time to the compelling beat with such faultless style and rhythm that she knew, with a swift and total change of opinion, that she could not have expected anything less from him. Music was in his blood, whether it was produced by the great orchestras or the frankly commercial interests of the pop world he was bound to respond.

And she felt very grateful for the occasional opportunities she had had to brush up her disco dancing. It had been something her aunt, greatly indulgent, had encouraged when they had been on board ship, although Krista doubted that she would have approved equally the less inhibited exhibitionism of some of the customers here. She tried not to see the couple next to them, who were kissing with increasing passion at each throbbing forceful beat of the music, tried to edge round a bit, excluding their entwined bodies from her vision, but a raised eyebrow from Ludovic, a flickering glance over her head, told her that he was well aware of what she was about. It was as well when the music ended, just in time she thought as she caught sight of the bewildered, glazed look in the eyes of the girl who had been forced to release her partner, but it was a relief for her to feel Ludovic's arm about her as he led her in the direction of one of the ante-rooms.

'Come on, Krista.' Gratefully she leaned against him, while her blood pressure, increased by the exertion of the prolonged session slowly returned to normal, happy when she realised they had come into a small bar where soft drinks were available.

An iced Coke was just what she wanted. She watched him pull the tab from his tin and put it to his lips before following his example. She had never thought much of the habit of drinking straight from a tin, but this was neither the time nor the place for Edinburgh 'niceness' and she found it easier than she had imagined.

'You look hot.' Ludovic put up a hand to touch her flushed face which was no help in cooling her down.

'And you,' Krista struggled against the surge of discomfort in the pit of her stomach, an emotion she was all too sure would find further reflection in her blazing cheeks, 'you look as cool as you always do.'

'Do I?' His blue eyes blazed down at her for a

moment, then narrowed, cooled, and his white smile dismissed any idea of emotional involvement. 'But looks can be so deceptive, can they not, *drágám*?'

'Can they?' She tried to be casual and just a little sophisticated. 'Are you telling me that you're burning with passion inside while you preserve that cool exterior?'

'I might be.' He grinned as if he understood everything about her. 'You should know, Krista,' the way he spoke her name always gave her this deep-down throb and perversely she felt a flash of indignation that he persisted in using it. Then as if reading her mind again he changed the subject. He had manoeuvred her into a corner, away from the worst of the throng, supporting himself with one hand against the black wall while she leaned against it looking up at him. 'But tell me, how do you come to be such a disco expert?'

Daringly she made a face at him. 'Why not?'

His eyes never left her face as he drank again from the tin. 'It's just so . . . unexpected.'

'Is it? What kind of dancing did you think I *would* be expert in? The valeta, perhaps? Or even the minuet?'

He shook his head without answering, but his eyes were full of strange messages which had her heart palpitating against her ribs. Then the hand which had been supporting him against the wall moved and pulled the scarf from her hair. Instinctively she murmured a protest, but he quickly held it away from her, beyond her reach.

'Leave your hair.' He stopped the hand as it went up to straighten her disordered tresses. 'I like it as it is.' He pushed the scarf into the pocket of his lightweight jacket which he took off and slung over his arm. 'Shall we dance again?'

'Yes.' Following his example, Krista placed her empty tin on a shelf that ran round the wall and turned again towards the dance floor where again all the customers were twisting in time to the beat.

'Give me your jacket.' It didn't occur to her that it was a subject on which she was quite capable of making up her own mind, and obediently she shrugged herself out of the safari jacket which was tossed, with his own, on a convenient chair.

There was little doubt that she felt much freer in the sleeveless camisole blouse, much more comfortable as she raised her arms, snapped her fingers. And in the flashing lights she could even admire the golden honey tan of her skin, the way the fine hair gleamed softly on her forearms.

Ludovic too appeared to find the change agreeable; there was a half-smile on his lips, while his eyes were blatantly approving her smooth shoulders and neck, bare but for the slender silver chain she wore.

It was late when finally the music ended and along with dozens of other they stood for a few moments in the darkness outside, savouring the sudden quiet while hearts and souls still throbbed to the music.

It seemed natural when his arm came round her shoulders, pulling her close to him as slowly they walked back to where they had left the car outside the *auberge*.

'Are you tired, *drágám*?' The powerful fingers cut into the flesh of her upper arm.

'I ought to be,' she smiled. 'I was before. So why is it that I feel so alive now? When we've been dancing like dervishes for the last ... how long, Ludovic?'

'Two,' a quick glance at his watch, 'no, three hours.'

'Oh!' It was close to a groan. 'And you have all that way to drive back, Ludovic.'

'Ah . . .' He seemed to hesitate, then swung her round to face him. 'Ah,' he said again, and brushed a strand of hair back from her face with a sensitive, ice-trickling finger, 'there I have a confession, Krista. You will not be angry, I hope?'

'Angry?' Wide grey eyes stared up at him. 'Angry?' Her laugh was brief, not quite certain. 'I can't imagine what you could do to make me angry, Ludovic, but . . .'

'Ssh!' There was a touch of lips against hers, faint but enough to make further words fly from her mind. 'Ssh, Krista.' He spoke as softly as if they were in danger of being overheard. 'Don't say anything to modify that statement. Only, some time ago, before even we went in to the restaurant to have dinner, I arranged that we should stay the night in the *auberge*.'

'Stay the night?' Shock made her eyes widen further, again she felt surges of totally novel emotions threaten to overwhelm her. What could he mean? Was it . . .

'There you go again, repeating what I say!' But there was none of the acerbity that had coloured the same comment earlier that day. Instead a mellowness seemed to have overtaken him, a gentleness which made him brush one hand against her cheek, then almost experimentally repeat the action. 'Yes, stay the night.' He put a hand to the pocket of his jacket where she heard metals clink. 'I arranged it all when I first spoke to the *patron*. Here, I have the keys.'

Apparently that was all the explanation he considered necessary, for they turned and strolled on in the direction of their hotel. Ludovic seemed to be calm enough. Even in the midst of her distracting thoughts that was a point she could recognise. He was cool, calm and collected just because the situation was one in which he was entirely at ease. But she—she couldn't even think. Why, why hadn't she guessed that this might be in his mind? Bringing her all this way, pretending that he wanted to escape from the pressures for a day. And all the time he had been planning—*this*.

But, as they walked along in the gentle silence, the only sounds made by their footfalls on the cobbled road, some sense of moderation returned to her. It was idiotic to think that he had planned it all like Napoleon and his Russian campaign. It was probably much more casual, an idea that had occurred to him just as they had made their way into the town. What more natural, for a man like him, to see the disco, decide they could spend a few hours there, return to the *auberge* to spend the night. Together! It was supposed to be the perfect way to relax, wasn't it? She had read that somewhere. Panic began to mount inside her again. But that presupposed a certain amount of experience on both sides. She didn't imagine that it was quite the same thing with a girl like her, one who until now had never had the slightest inclination to do . . .

'Here we are.' Gently he disengaged himself from her while he fished in his pocket for the key to open the locked front door of the *auberge*. 'Would you like some coffee, Krista?' The soft vibrance of his voice as they stood close together in the dimness of the foyer did nothing to cool her, so she contented herself with a swift shake of the head. He smiled, dangled the keys tantalisingly in front of her so that she could see quite easily the number of the room on the metal tag which held both keys together.

If he noticed her trembling as they walked
together up the steep crooked stair he gave no sign
but stopped at room number six and slid the
smaller of the keys into the lock. Krista stood in
the open doorway and when his finger had
touched the switch operating the lamps, saw the
large bed spread with a rich tapestry counterpane,
expensive-looking lamps with silk shades, tinted
glass mirrors set in rococo frames.

One of these showed her own reflection, her hair
spilling in an unruly mass about her shoulders,
wide eyes, full soft mouth not quite managing to
hide her innocence. The pale safari suit showed the
length of her slim legs, but nervously her fingers
went out to pull the open edges of her jacket more
closely about her.

Unwillingly her eyes moved to the dark outline
behind her. Ludovic's eyes had never seemed more
threatening, more conscious of her vulnerability,
more determined to take what he wanted. Yet
when he spoke his words were so matter-of-fact,
his tone so everyday that her fears seemed to be
rudely squashed.

'It is all right?'

'All right?' she echoed, watching him in the glass
without moving.

He smiled, trying to remind her of the habit he
pretended to dislike.

'The room. Is it all right, *drágám*?'

'Of course. The room is beautiful.' When she
realised he was about to brush past her she
launched herself into a gabble. 'I would never have
thought that a small *auberge* like this would have
such luxurious bedrooms.'

If he heard her Ludovic gave no sign but tried a
door and gave a grunt of satisfaction as it opened
on to a tiled bathroom. Then he answered her

comment. 'Oh, it is usual enough. Besides, they have three stars for cooking and the rooms merely follow.' He returned to where she was still standing in the open doorway. 'I shouldn't have a bath tonight, *drágám*. It might disturb the other guests.'

'No. All right.' Huge eyes refused to look directly at him.

'So. *Bonsoir.*'

'*Bonsoir?*' She couldn't quite keep the surprised query from her voice.

Ludovic grinned as if she had made some rather sophisticated joke. 'Yes, it is a pity, is it not, Krista?' Then quite suddenly the smile faded, his eyebrows came down together in a frown of speculation. 'If I didn't know otherwise I might imagine that you were making some sort of proposition!' Swiftly he dropped a kiss on her cheek. 'I must not even suggest such a thing or you will be horrified to the depths of your presbyterian soul. Besides, I would hate to do anything which might damage the relationship we have with each other, Krista. And of course there is ...' He frowned quite ferociously for an instant, then Krista felt herself being thrust inside the door which was firmly closed between them.

For a long time she just stood where he had left her, feeling all the excitement, all the joy, all the wild wonder and anticipation slowly ebb, leaving, in place of the glowing flesh and blood she had been, an empty husk. You could see, she thought as she took a step towards the smoked glass, you could see she was a different person from the one who had stood there when the lights had flicked on.

Impulsively she threw her jacket from her shoulders on to the bed, raked her fingers through her hair so that it stood out even more wildly than before. Even with her Kate Bush hairstyle she had lost her vitality. Now the mouth drooped the eyes were heavy with fatigue, reminding her of how utterly exhausted she was. Now all she had to do was slip beneath the sheets and drift away into sleep.

But for hours she lay in the darkness longing for oblivion, almost weeping with frustration that sleep should have become so elusive. Then she gave up the pretence when she realised that each time she closed her eyes she saw Ludovic etched on her eyelids, coming towards her, arms outstretched. And somehow the fact that she was sleeping with no clothes did nothing to calm her fevered longings, not even an underskirt between her and these ridiculous, utterly uncharacteristic feelings.

Trying to force her mind on to a cool and cooling self-analysis, she began to take herself back to Edinburgh, already assuming a distant, a foreign image in her mind after the few months of travel. She thought of Iain, summoning his features to her mind's eye only after a considerable amount of almost desperate concentration. Then when he was fixed, his nondescript colouring, halfway between ginger and fair, seemed such an utter contradiction of everything she had ever considered attractive that she was inclined to abandon the exercise then and there.

Only the deep-down realisation that she must fill her thoughts with what was wholesome, what was possible, kept her on course, and she recalled with a pang of guilt how unfeeling she had been towards him the last time they had met. She hadn't known then ... Even when she had decided she was leaving Edinburgh with Ludovic she hadn't taken the trouble to let him know. It was the awful accusation he had made which had stopped her when once or twice she had picked up the telephone with the intention of ringing his number.

'You couldn't keep your eyes off the conductor fellow in there!' In anger at her rebuff he had thrown the words at her. And in anger her hand had come out and struck him. As she lay in the darkness of the room in Massian her face burning at the recollection, a sob burst from her lips. How could she have done such a thing? She and Iain Melville had been friends for years, and surely it was a compliment if a man liked you enough to want to marry you. Oh, if only she could have felt the same way how easy life would have been!

'You couldn't keep your eyes off that conductor fellow.' Iain's words refused to be excluded from her mind, forcing her to recognise how it always came back to that. And suddenly everything was as clear as day to her.

It had been true. Even then it had been true, and all this time she had been fooling herself.

Long, long ago when she had thought of marriage it had been impossible to think of Iain, less still Hamish, as lovers. Even with the wedding ring firmly pushed on to her finger she had found the contemplation of such circumstances singularly unappealing. And yet tonight, walking back from the disco with Ludovic, she had been perfectly willing to fall in with whatever plans he had for bringing the evening to a perfect conclusion and with no thoughts of wedding rings in her mind.

Willing? She allowed herself a tiny sardonic grimace. Don't kid yourself any longer, Krista. You might have been trying to pretend you were willing. But such a milk-and-water feeling could not explain away the despair that had flooded her body when the door closed behind him.

No, she had been eager to believe Ludovic
wanted her to spend the night with him. If she
hadn't been quite so eager then she would not so
instantly have jumped to the wrong conclusion.
After all, they had spent many nights together in
the same hotel, why should this one have been so
very different?

And then to be so foolish as to let him have
some glimpse of what she was expecting. He had
carried it off very well, but then he did most
things well. But that little laugh at what he
pretended was a bit of her teasing had been a
perfect touch, ensuring that neither of them
would feel embarrassed in the morning. Ensuring
too—it was a bleak thought—that his rejection
need not be too bruising. He must have had
plenty of practice at extricating himself from
females who threw themselves at him. The ones
he didn't fancy, that was.

Then there was something else he had said. If
she racked her brains it would come back. Oh yes.
'I would hate anything to damage our relationship.'
That again was a clever balm for her protection,
but then he had made that curious half-statement.
'And of course there is . . .'

The solution to that cryptic comment came to
her even when she wasn't looking for it. 'Of course
there is the woman I love. There is Barbe.'

That was it. Quite simple when you tried to
think things through to their logical conclusion.
Numbly she lay in the aching darkness.

'You can't keep your eyes off that conductor
fellow.' If it hadn't been true then, her reaction
would have been less exaggerated.

But like almost every other female she had
been aware of him even before they had
exchanged a dozen words. She had been half in

love with him when he forced her to walk round
the garden after the ghastly scene with Iain. And
sadly, she had never been one to do things by
halves. Krista put her head into her pillow and
wept.

CHAPTER SIX

THEY arrived back at the château in the middle of the morning, Ludovic insisting they should go there first before they drove on to the hotel. Their meeting at breakfast had been unremarkable, and Krista took care to wear her dark glasses indoors in case he made any remark about her swollen eyes. However, his glance in her direction was brief indeed when she found him studying a newspaper while he drank his coffee and in the face of such uncomplicated normality her tendency towards the emotional could hardly be sustained.

But when they stopped the car in front of the imposing building tension began to mount inside her again, increased when she caught sight of Barbe break off a conversation she was having with one of the gardeners in the rose garden and come towards them. There was something in her manner, perhaps it was in the short purposeful strides, heels tapping busily on the mellow paving that was a warning to Krista, but there was little in her greeting to Ludovic that would have raised any eyebrows.

Although to begin with his manner would have discouraged any criticism, for he raised one foot onto the low balustrade and leaned forward, smiling as he watched the Comtesse climb the few steps to their level.

'*Bonjour*, Barbe.' One dark arm swept round in a grand gesture like those he made when he was conducting, Krista thought. 'How beautiful the garden looks in the sunshine.' And you too, the warmth in his voice might have been saying.

'*Bonjour, chéri.*' The dark flashing eyes lost a little of their verve when they moved beyond Ludovic to where Krista, feeling very much an unnecessary spectator of the scene, was standing. 'I am so pleased you are back.' There was scarcely a shade of criticism in her voice. 'Our guests were so disappointed that you were not here to say goodbye to them yesterday.'

He shrugged and smiled, covering the hand she had slipped into his arm with long dark fingers. 'But I know you understand, Barbe. After the tensions of a concert I decided I had to get away. My letter reached you safely?'

'Yes.' A pause while she smiled up at him, forgiveness in the limpid brilliance of her eyes. 'Only I did not expect you to remain away overnight.'

'No, that was unplanned. It was simply that when we had eaten we were too tired to make the long drive home.'

When he said 'we' Barbe's reaction was much more subtle than Krista's had been the previous night. Seeing the slightly narrowed eyes, immediately retracted, the unwavering smile the younger girl could not withhold a ripple of admiration. The Comtesse had simply had the sense, the patience to wait for the information to be revealed, without having to show her own interest. Until Ludovic had told her so, she had been silently wondering if he had gone off on his own. Or had the British girl been with him?

There was a second's pause, so brief that surely only the two woman were aware that it had happened, before Barbe went on with the assurance which Krista had already noticed.

'Of course.' The small hand moved against his, causing Krista to avert her eyes with a stab of sheer jealousy. 'Of course, *chéri*. But now all the guests have gone and you can have all the peace you want.' She paused. 'And Krista's room is waiting for her again. It was so good of you to move out, but now I shall send to the hotel to have your cases brought back.'

'Oh, thank you, Comtesse.' Studiously Krista avoided looking at her hostess. 'But I shall have to go back myself and make sure everything is properly packed.'

'Surely,' she smiled quite as if she had not virtually ejected Krista from the château, 'surely you did not unpack everything for just one night?'

Forcing herself to take her time, Krista looked calmly at the Comtesse, decided not to answer directly, then sensing without really seeing the other woman's fingers link round Ludovic's, she changed the subject abruptly.

'I must go and check on the arrangements for Wednesday's concert. If you will permit me, Comtesse.'

'Naturellement.' Barbe showed her small white teeth in a smile that told Krista all too clearly that she considered she had won this particular encounter. And when she reached the small study which had been put at their disposal for the period of their stay she reached for the file and went through the pretence of checking things which had already been checked and re-checked for the informal concert arranged at very short notice.

Fauré's Requiem. She put a large tick against the first item for the recital, which was being given by the orchestra and choir of the local high school. Next on the all-French programme, excerpts from a ballet suite by Chabrier and lastly Bolero by

Ravel which Ludovic always referred to as the pot-boiler.

All the ticking completed, Krista sat down on a chair by the window looking out to where she had left them a few moments earlier. They were no longer in sight, but a flash of pink among the trees the colour of the dress Barbe had been wearing gave some indication of the direction they had taken. Even now he might have his arms about her, holding her close to him while he smiled down into her animated face. He might be . . .

She put a hand to her eyes in a gesture of despair, wishing she could blot out the scenes that seemed to keep floating into her vision with such distracting persistence. Ludovic might even now be asking her to marry him, insisting that their engagement should be announced without further delay. There must, *must* be more in their relationship than mere friendship. After all—her eyes were drawn again to the open file—a man as frantically busy as Ludovic Hasek doesn't come all this way, give his services free to amateur orchestras unless he has some very good reason for doing so. And what better reason could there be than to give pleasure to the woman he loved?

Krista closed the file and got up with an air of great determination. She had to grit her teeth and face the facts. As far as Ludovic was concerned she was just his secretary. Anything else that might have squeezed into their relationship was simply a result of his basic kindness, and she would be foolish to get the wrong end of the stick. Even when he had taken her away from Edinburgh that had probably been a case of pity. The realisation brought a bleakness to her eyes.

Now the only thing she could do was to put up with the situation as it now existed. She would go and get her cases from the hotel, it would do no good to make a fuss and say she preferred to remain there. She would bring her things back to the château, and no matter how subtly the Comtesse tried to show how unwelcome she found her presence, Krista decided her own reaction must be passive.

But it seemed that Krista had made a mistake about Barbe, for the older woman's manner was friendly, affectionate even, when the three of them met in the small dining room for lunch later that day. Naturally Krista ascribed her change of manner to the happiness caused by her approaching engagement, and her own determination to hide her feelings of despair were redoubled.

'Now,' Barbe was almost playful as she smiled across the round table at her guest, 'I hope you have a really pretty dress with you, Krista.'

'A pretty dress?' As she raised her head from the delicious salad Krista imagined she intercepted a secretive glance between her two companions. 'I . . . I don't understand what you mean, Comtesse.' She wondered if her face had paled betrayingly.

'Oh, why do you insist on being so formal?' Barbe protested mildly. 'A pretty dress,' she repeated. 'I feel so sad that you had to miss our reception the other evening.' The black eyes looking across at Krista were innocent of guilt, the words implying that it had been entirely the other girl's choice to be absent. 'And so tonight I have decided to have a tiny dinner party.' Her expression grew even more gentle as she glanced at Ludovic. 'Jean-Paul wishes to meet you again. And it will be much more fun for a young girl than a stuffy reception.' Her words seemed chosen to give the impression that Krista was little more than a schoolgirl.

'I'm sorry you have had to go to so much trouble, Barbe.' Anger at her hostess had to be controlled, but nevertheless her voice shook a little and certainly she avoided looking in the direction of her employer.

'Nonsense, my dear.' The tone suggested she would go to any lengths to make sure Krista had a good time. 'Why should I not do this little thing for you? It gives me pleasure, so I will hear no more protests. Only I want to know if you have a pretty dress. If anything needs ironing then give it to Hortense after luncheon and she will see to it. We want you to look your prettiest, do we not, Ludovic?'

At last Krista could not resist looking at him, knowing well enough that she had been the subject of his scrutiny since their hostess had begun the conversation. And the expression she met in those startling dark blue eyes reminded her of an occasion right at the beginning of their acquaintance, before even they had spoken to each other. Then there had been a kind of appraising curiosity at once shrouded by the thick lashes concealing his expression. As now.

'Of course.' His reply was bland, unemotional, so that quite illogically she was stung to the quick. In disgust her eyes flicked from him to her hostess and she smiled falsely.

'Yes, as it happens I do have a dress, one which I haven't had the opportunity to wear. I shall look forward to dressing up tonight. Thank you, Barbe.'

It was a shock to discover when she put on the dress later that evening that the back zip could be pulled up only with difficulty. All that fattening French food, she told herself, with a promise that soon she would try to get rid of the few extra

pounds. Not that the appearance of the dress was
affected. It was as gorgeous as she had remembered
and she couldn't imagine why she hadn't worn it
before. Yes, she could. She had been saving it for
some spectacularly special occasion. What that
occasion might be she wasn't prepared to admit even
to herself. Certainly not Ludovic's engagement to
someone else. But if that did happen this evening,
then the dress and knowing she looked her best
would give her the confidence to carry it off.

Black suited her. And it certainly went with her
mood, even though that didn't show. She forced
her mind back towards her appearance, admiring
the neat tight bodice, the way it showed off both
curves and small waist, the deep square neckline
drawing attention to her honey-coloured skin. The
frothy sleeves were elbow-length with a deep lacy
frill and the filmy chiffon was embroidered with
shining bugles. Round her neck she wore a
necklace of moonstones, a gift her uncle had
brought with him from Australia, and matching
drop earrings.

The dress was calf-length and the high-heeled
black sandals would, she thought, give her a
decided psychological advantage over Barbe. That
and the way her grey eyes had been enchanced by
some subtle green shadow and the full mouth
coloured by a browny pink gloss. There too she
had an advantage over Barbe, whose only flaw
was that her lips were rather thin.

If she had had any doubts about her appearance
they would have been swept away by the
expression she saw on Ludovic's face when she
went downstairs. He was passing through the hall
at the time and Krista paused a few steps from the
bottom, one hand resting on the banister while
they stood looking at each other.

There was nothing hidden in his startled expression, and Krista felt all determination to remain aloof and detached swept aside in a single breathless second.

'Krista—*drágám*!' He took a step towards her, one hand held out.

But before she could raise her fingers towards his the familiar sound of footsteps echoing on the marble floor returned her to her senses. She smiled coolly, disguised the pang when she saw his hand drop to his side and looked up as their hostess tap-tapped her way across the hall.

The flicker of suspicion on Barbe's face was immediately expunged as Ludovic turned to her, and replaced by a look of admiration. 'How pretty you look, Krista. Did I not tell you,' one proprietorial hand was slipped through his arm, 'did I not tell you, *chéri*, that she could look divine?'

The patronising condescension made Krista's cheeks burn while a quick glance confirmed that the lovely black and silver dress might just be a little elaborate for a quiet dinner at home. Which naturally was exactly what Barbe had planned. When she had spoken about a 'pretty dress' she must have hoped that Krista would overdo it, and of course she had jumped into the trap prepared for her. Meantime Barbe had gone to the other extreme with expensive simplicity.

She too was in black, a long hostess gown high at the neck and with wrist-length tight sleeves, her only jewellery a long rope of pearls with small clusters in her ears. It was a totally effective look, emphasising her petite figure and making Krista, by clever contrast, feel gauche and clumsy.

But there was nothing she could do about it now, so bravely she raised her chin and came

down the few remaining steps, smiling her wholly
synthetic friendliness. 'Thank you, Barbe.' Then
she followed the tiny figure of her hostess and the
tall commanding figure of her employer across to
the reception room from which issued the sounds
of subdued laughter and the clink of glasses.

'Krista!' Jean-Paul, showing every sign of being
pleased to see her, rose from his chair and coming
towards her kissed her on both cheeks. 'You look
quite beautiful, *chérie*.' He caught both of her
hands and held them away from her sides. 'Does
she not, Barbe?' There was a suggestion of
mischief in the glance darted towards his sister,
then denying her the opportunity to reply,
'Ludovic?'

'Yes, quite beautiful,' Ludovic agreed without
looking at her again.

'Now you must come and meet our friends,
Krista.' Barbe put a firm hand on her elbow and
went through the formalities, introducing her to a
youngish couple who were sitting side by side on a
green and gold antique sofa. 'Max and Bernice
Rambeau.' Krista smiled and offered a hand to
each of them. The woman, she was pleased to see,
was wearing a dress closer to her own in style than
to Barbe's. 'And of course you know Philippe.'
And the young man who had joined her for dinner
the other night got up from his seat close to the
door, smiled at her, cradled her fingertips in his
hand for a moment before taking them to his lips.

'Of course.' Philippe's eyes were even more
admiring than they had been in the Cheval Blanc,
and Krista was so shocked by his unexpected
appearance that she didn't snatch her hand away
as quickly as she might have done. She was too
busy casting a guilty glance in Ludovic's direction.

And he, of course, in spite of the way he was

casually involved in a conversation with the Rambeaus, had his eyes on what was happening over by the door. Krista felt the warm colour burn her skin, saw his eyes narrow as they glanced from her to Philippe and back again. And only then did she pull her fingers from the other's man's clasp.

Why, oh, why, she asked herself as course followed interminable course, didn't I tell Ludovic that I had dinner with Philippe the other night? I had the opportunity, there's no use pretending I didn't. Only I deliberately decided to let him think I'd been on my own all evening. Playing for his sympathy, perhaps, or hoping that he would blame Barbe—oh, I don't know why, what I wanted him to think. And heaven knows what he's thinking now. She looked up, interrupting a dark brooding expression in his eyes, an expression he showed no willingness to withdraw, so that she was the first to look elsewhere.

'Krista . . .' Barbe's voice was amused, patient. 'Bernice was asking you a question, *chérie*!'

'I'm sorry.' Fingers reaching in confusion for her glass shook, splashing the wine, her dismay mounted as the dark stain spread over the perfect whiteness of the cloth, but any hope that the little accident might have escaped notice was dashed as she saw satisfaction flash for an instant in Barbe's eyes. It was that expression that killed the apology which it would have been natural in the circumstances to make. 'I'm sorry, Bernice, I was miles away.' But despite all her efforts her smile was taut and strained.

'I was asking you,' Bernice's smile showed some sympathy, her eyes were warm and understanding, 'if you would be going to New York with Ludovic. He has just been telling us that his next commitments are in Edinburgh and the States.'

'New York?' she repeated stupidly, praying that her employer would come to her aid, that he would let her as well as the others sitting round the table know just what she was to expect in the weeks and months ahead. 'I'm ... I'm not certain. It will depend. You see, Jerzy is ...'

'Krista hasn't yet made up her mind.' At last the smooth mellow voice broke in. 'There are so many things to be considered. In the first place, I had the utmost difficulty in persuading her aunt to allow her to come away with me in the first place. Before any decision can be made then Lady James will have to be consulted.' His manner, the way he looked at her and smiled, easy, friendly, made her heart flip over, restored some of her confidence.

'So,' it was Philippe, mildly teasing who drew her attention now, 'you must have your aunt's permission before you can decide these things.'

'How sweet!' Barbe's comment to which surely no one could have taken the slightest exception made Krista fume with anger. Sparks flew from her eyes as she looked at her hostess, but then something, possibly the least little move of Ludovic's hand as he took his glass to his lips, made her look at him. And she remembered her resolution, that she would be perfectly polite to the woman in whose house they were staying, the woman he might be planning to marry. No one would have guessed how a knife turned in her chest as she smiled.

'I suppose it seems strange nowadays,' her smile encompassed them all and even saved a little for self-mockery, 'but I do owe a great deal to my aunt. In spite of what some people think,' she allowed herself the tiny indulgence of an innocent, wide-eyed look at Ludovic, 'she and I are very good friends. And she wouldn't dream of stopping

me doing what I want to do. She's just,' now that
the words had started it was surprising how easily
they flowed, 'like many men. If guided in the right
direction she will eventually come up with a
wonderful idea—and never even wonder where
the idea came from in the first place.'

There was a murmur of amusement and Jean-
Paul, who was sitting next to her, covered one of
her hands with his. 'I should not have thought you
would be so devious, *chérie*.' The warm, surprisingly
benevolent dark eyes caressed her. 'So beautiful,'
he shook his head, 'and yet so devious.'

'And I was told you were an expert on women
Jean-Paul.' The sophisticated little drawl in her
voice did something for her self-esteem.

'But I am, Krista.' There was a practised throb
in his deep voice. 'And you never cease to surprise
me.' He took her fingers to his mouth, kissed the
tips before gently releasing them. Krista discovered
that she was much, much less sophisticated than
she had imagined.

Later, when they were sitting round the large
coffee table in the salon, Krista found Philippe
beside her on the long sofa, his manner much more
intimate than it had been two nights earlier, so
familiar indeed that once or twice Ludovic looked
across at them from his position on Barbe's left
with an enquiring raised eyebrow. Krista, finding
some relief in the situation, perhaps even hoping
that her behaviour might cause Ludovic one or
two pangs of jealousy, responded to Philippe's
flattery, and when Jean-Paul came to perch on the
arm of the sofa she had no qualms about flirting
with both of them.

There was music from a hi-fi concealed
somewhere in the region of a large elaborately
carved cabinet, and it wasn't long before it became

obvious that the orchestra was one that had
Ludovic as conductor. Krista allowed the soft
conversation to wash past her, as the liquid notes
of Beethoven's Moonlight Sonata fell softly in the
room. But when she saw Barbe lay her head on
Ludovic's shoulder, sigh and slip her hand into
his, Krista found she was straining to hear their
low voices. To increase her difficulties they were
speaking in French, but even so, it was clear
enough that they were remembering another time
when they had listened together to the music.
Barbe was assuring him that it was an evening she
would remember always, to the end of her life.

And if Ludovic's response was less emotional,
then there was no doubt he was willing enough to
be taken back to that time; the smile on his face,
the gentleness of his expression was quite explicit.

Suddenly the music lost all its appeal for Krista,
and when the record ended, before another could
replace it she rose and walked over to the long
window, looking out on to the darkened garden
but seeing only the reflection of the room on
which she had turned her back. Jean-Paul raised a
cynical mocking eyebrow at his sister before he got
up and strolled over to study a collection of
colourful china in one of the glass-fronted
cabinets. Then Philippe, after what seemed to be a
long non-productive look at his hostess, rose and
crossed to the window to join Krista.

It was too late for her to escape whatever her
inclination, it would look too pointed to turn away
the moment he came up to her. Besides, she didn't
know if that was what she wanted. At least with
someone to talk to she could pretend that her
feelings of self-pity and neglect didn't exist. So she
responded to his touch with a welcoming smile.

'You did not enjoy the music, Krista?'

'Yes, I did. Only that particular piece always makes me sad.'

'I understand, and agree with you. You were not, I hope, wishing yourself to be back in Scotland?'

'Of course not!' The denial came quickly enough, but could not wholly dismiss the idea that maybe he had hit the nail on the head. This aching feeling, this feeling of emptiness could be something as simple as homesickness. Why on earth hadn't that solution occurred to her before? A sob of misery rose in her throat, was immediately stifled, but still showed in the brilliance in her eyes. She ought to be back in Edinburgh. What was she doing here among people with whom she had nothing in common?

She blinked, looking away from her companion towards where Barbe and Ludovic were sitting close together on the sofa. But he at least was distracted, his eyes were fixed firmly on Krista as if he disapproved of her standing talking so intimately with the young Frenchman. Immediately her attention was transferred, and the smile she turned on Philippe was a blatant invitation.

But in spite of the lighthearted conversation in which they indulged it was impossible for Krista to throw off the feelings of home-or-some-other-kind of sickness which had assaulted her with such suddenness. It was the first time since her journeyings across Europe had begun that she had yearned for what was familiar and a trifle dull. But with each passing second she became more conscious of being out of her element. As she chatted and smiled at Philippe she found her eyes constantly drawn to the pair on the sofa, seeing, envying Barbe's perfect self-assurance, acknowledging with bitter self-flagellation that

she would make a superb wife for a man in the
public eye.

Whereas she, she was little more than the wide-
eyed innocent she had been three months ago. In
spite of the air of sophistication she was learning
to assume, take away all the glitter of new clothes,
the glamour of her surroundings and she was very
much the same as she had always been. It wasn't
even as if she knew a great deal about music. No,
her value to Ludovic was the fact that she could
type, do some filing and keep track of all the
arrangements that had to be made. She was a
moderately efficient P.A.

'Why don't you leave the old trout and come
away with me?' He had laughed down at her, the
dark eyes challenging that evening in Aunt Diana's
drawing room.

'Oh, I couldn't possibly, Mr Hasek.' It was the
most polished reply she could think of at the time.
Nevertheless she had come, exchanging one kind
of slavery for another. Self-pity racked her again.

'Krista!' There was a shade of reproach in
Philippe's voice and she realised that for the last
few moments she had lost track of his teasing
comments.

'I'm sorry.' She blushed a little and gave him all
her attention, leaning back against the heavy
curtains, allowing him to put an arm on the wall
behind her, to bend over her, smiling his continued
admiration.

'You were miles away.'

'Not really.' she lied easily.

'I was asking,' his voice was low and intimate,
'if you would have dinner with me tomorrow
night.'

'Oh,' instantly she regretted that she had given
him so much encouragement, 'I don't think I can,

Philippe, thank you. I just don't know what the plans are for tomorrow.'

'But you must!' he protested, and his voice became a shade more positive. 'The other night,' a hand came out, a sensitive finger traced the line of her cheek, 'meant so much to me. I could not believe my luck when you permitted me to join you.'

Suddenly Krista found herself looking over Philippe's shoulder and into dark blue eyes which showed their displeasure and almost at the same moment Philippe appeared to become aware that they had been joined by a third person, for he laughed a little selfconsciously, his hand dropped to his side and he included Ludovic in his plea.

'I have been asking Krista if she will dine with me tomorrow evening.'

'Really?' Ludovic did not as much as glance at the man, all his attention, all his annoyance were reserved for his secretary. 'And Krista has said——?' He took his cheroot from his mouth, blowing the smoke away from them. Krista was unable to take her eyes from the long slim fingers, she was fascinated by the well-kept fingernails, the sprinkling of dark hair on the skin. 'Krista?' he repeated with the impatience she knew only too well.

'Yes?' Her voice told him that she too could be erratic and unreasonable—was intended to tell him exactly that.

'You have had an invitation. I was asking what your reply had been.'

'I've refused it.' She forced the cool answer from her lips, but considered there was no need to explain any further. Only she had reckoned without Philippe.

'Krista seems to have the idea that you will object.'

'Krista is a free agent.' For the first time he looked directly at the other man, but there was no hint of friendliness in his manner.

'Then, *chérie*,' if Philippe noticed any coolness in Ludovic's attitude he gave no sign but turned to Krista with increased pleading, 'please say you will come. I enjoyed it so much the other evening. And you did too.' There was a subtle change in his voice, it grew more intimate, almost as if he had forgotten Ludovic's presence. 'You told me so.'

Krista could not quite subdue the blush that coloured her cheeks, but her mind was a confusion of indecision. One part of her was pleased—*pleased* Ludovic need not think she was totally dependent on him for her relaxation, but on the other hand, she knew he would be furious to think that she had deceived him about the evening she had spent at the Cheval Blanc. When they had been at the beach yesterday she had had the ideal opportunity to tell him about Philippe. But she had funked it. Well, why shouldn't she? She didn't have to account to him for every single moment of her time. She was too old for a nanny. And a nanny who was standing glowering at her, simmering with anger did not come into her scheme of things.

'Well, thank you, Philippe.' She smiled up at him but still could not bring herself to promise him a whole evening of her time. There was something about him, about that fortuitous meeting the other night which struck her as just a little bit odd. 'May I think about it? I have masses of work to do tomorrow.' Her sweet smile was meant to imply great patience in the face of callous exploitation. 'But if I'm not too exhausted then of course I'd love to come with you. Perhaps if you could ring about five I could let you know . . .'

'*Bien.*' There was a satisfied expression on his face as he gave a brief formal bow, quite at variance with the familiar way he had been stroking her cheek seconds before.

'Then ...' Krista gave a breathless little laugh, 'I think I'll just ask Barbe if she'll excuse me. I've had a few hectic days and I feel exhausted. Besides,' she couldn't resist the last gibe at Ludovic, 'I hardly slept at all last night.'

Only when she reached her room did she allow herself to relax, to incline wearily against the closed door for a moment before walking forward to the long mirror where she could face herself. It was a surprise to find she looked much the same as she had when she went down this evening. None of the harrowing feelings she had endured had etched the marks of suffering on her face. A hand went up to confirm what her eyes told her and a tiny smile curved her mouth.

It was only then that recollection of that first night returned to her, stirred into life again by the words that had come into her mind downstairs. But it was another scene from that occasion which came back to haunt her now as she remembered how Jane McDonald had looked while she had flirted with Ludovic. She had been wearing a dress very like this, black and filmy with touches of gold and shiny black sequins. Was it possible—Krista's dark eyes searched her features for a denial—was it possible that even then she had been jealous of any attention he paid to other women? No, her mind shrieked the word and she allowed herself to be convinced. That was just too much to believe.

Nevertheless, later on, when she had been tossing and turning in the comfortable bed for what seemed eternity, she found herself unable to accept the assurance so completely.

CHAPTER SEVEN

KRISTA was, to all appearances, totally absorbed by paperwork when Ludovic came into the office the following morning. Her response to his greeting was abstracted, too involved with worrying matters to spare much of her time for the niceties. Yet every inch of her was aware of him, feeling his usual throbbing vitality today heightened by a brooding intensity beating beneath the thin white shirt, always controlled but today only just.

'You did not eat breakfast this morning.' When he decided she was not going to speak he asked the question.

'No.' She flicked a cool glance approximately in his direction. 'I thought I'd told you, I'm trying to lose some weight.'

It annoyed her that he made no protest, no mention now of the perfect figure he had spoken of once or twice. Krista continued to scrutinise her notes making one or two meaningless squiggles on the pad, pretending not to see him perched on the corner of the desk, the long legs, feet enclosed in finest calfskin swinging gently.

'I think I ought to warn you, Krista ...' There was a frown in his voice which she knew would be repeated on his features if she took the trouble to look. But of course she wouldn't.

'Mmm,' she murmured vaguely, deliberately annoying.

'For God's sake will you put that down and listen to me!' He pulled the book from her fingers and stood up, glaring at her, the air of menace about him making the atmosphere in the room shimmer dangerously.

In spite of the trickle of apprehension that ran through her Krista continued the pretence that she was distracted by the complexities of the work in hand. 'What did you say, Ludovic?'

'I asked you——' he spoke slowly, with great deliberation that told her how close he was to losing his temper. Once or twice in the time since she had joined him she had seen it happen with someone else, each time heaving a sigh of relief that she wasn't involved. His eyes sparked, 'I asked you to put this down.' Rather aimlessly he waved the notebook in front of her before tossing it on to the desk. 'I can't see what you have to do that is taking up so much of your time.'

'Well, that's as it should be.' Her voice was matter-of-fact, tolerant, equable, extremely irritating. 'That's why I'm here after all—to relieve you of all the drudgery of the arrangements.' With a harassed hand she pushed back the hair from her face, then reached out towards the abandoned notebook—and stopped. 'You were going to say something to me, Ludovic. What was it? A change you want me to make in the plans for tomorrow's concert arrangements?'

The sheer antagonism which blazed from his eyes shook her, made her draw breath sharply. But it was gone so quickly that she wondered if she had imagined it. Certainly his voice was equable enough.

'No. No change of plans. I'm sure the arrangements will be perfect—they usually are. That much I can say, Krista.'

The grudging note in his voice quenched any tendency to imagine she was being complimented, so she merely raised an eyebrow.

'It's about Duclos.'

'Duclos?' For a moment the name meant nothing to her, then, 'Do you mean Philippe?' The possibility that her behaviour the previous evening had got under his skin was a great deal more satisfying than she would have believed. 'What about him?' Her voice had just the right amount of amused curiosity.

'Of course I mean Philippe.' His tone conveyed something of his opinion of the young man. 'Who else do you know with that name?'

'I can't think of anyone else.' It was strange to feel so cool when he was uptight. Usually she reacted to his moods like a slow-burning fuse, but today . . . it hardly seemed to matter.

'That's what I imagined.' He paused, took a long leisurely look at her, his expression softening as the sun caught at the loose strands of gold hair, warmed the honey-coloured skin. 'About Philippe Duclos, Krista. I just hope that you won't take him too seriously.'

'Seriously . . .?' There was a scoffing note in her voice that made his eyes narrow. 'Why on earth should I take him seriously?'

'I don't know. But girls, especially girls like you, sometimes do.'

'Girls like me?' The phrase had excessive power to offend. 'What on earth do you mean by that? How am I different from any other girl?'

'That,' he spoke very slowly, as if he were speaking to himself and his eyes were very thoughtful, deep, intense and impossible to read, 'that, Krista, is what I keep asking myself.'

Time seemed to be suspended for a split second, Krista was aware of nothing but his nearness, the way light and sun seemed to cocoon them in a golden haze. Now was the time for her to say something soft, a few words which would meet him halfway, would deflect the irritation she had been so anxious to feed. 'I suppose you mean that I'm gauche, naïve, the exact opposite of . . .' As she bit off Barbe's name she pulled the typewriter towards her, rolling a sheet of paper into it, although she had no idea what she meant to type.

'That wasn't at all what I meant.' He sighed a little and moved away from her, going to stand by the window for a few silent seconds before turning back to her. 'All I'm trying to say is be careful. I should hate you to be hurt, *drágám*. Because of me.'

Something squeezed her heart when he said that, so that for a moment she could hardly breathe. But she bent over her machine, rubbing at a misplaced letter with an eraser. 'I shan't be hurt.' The ache in her chest increased. 'And if I am, it certainly won't be because of you, Ludovic.' In total defiance of every nerve in her body she was telling him he had no effect on her emotional life. She snatched the sheet of paper from her machine and stared at it with fascinated intensity. 'Oh, and don't worry about Philippe, because I very much doubt that I'll be accepting his invitation.'

'You won't?' There was no disguising the relief that sounded in his voice, and when she turned to look at him he was smiling at her, eyes as well as mouth. 'I'm glad, Krista. You see, when I found out that you had been seeing him I thought . . .'

'Oh, but I can explain that.' All at once the urge to tell everything of that chance meeting was to be delayed no longer. Comfort enveloped her like a warm beneficent atmosphere. 'You see, Ludovic . . .'

But at that very moment there was a brisk knock at the door and Barbe stood there, smiling at Ludovic, telling him that there was a call for him.

'Thanks, *chérie*.' His glance at Krista was warm, but when he left the two women together Krista had the very clear impression that her hostess had been listening at the door, ready to interrupt at whichever moment was calculated to cause most vexation.

Her smile at Krista was shrewd and calculating, and she perched on the corner of the desk where he had been sitting a moment before. 'It's such a relief to me, Krista ...' insincerity dripped from every word, 'such a relief to know that you look after Ludovic so well. I must confess,' she flicked an apologetic glance at the younger girl who was sitting motionless behind her machine, 'I confess when I first knew that Jerzy had let him down I was worried—very worried. And Ludovic must have realised how concerned I would be, and so he said nothing about it till you arrived. You would notice I was surprised to see you.'

'No.' It was easy to lie to Barbe. They both knew exactly what was meant. 'I didn't notice.'

'Well, I must be a good actress. But as I was saying, we have always been protective in our attitudes to each other. If I had known Jerzy had had to go off home I would have rushed over to Scotland to take over his duties.' It was difficult for Krista to imagine the Comtesse coping with all the boring details of his schedule, but she pretended to accept the tale. 'And that is why I want you to know how grateful I am, Krista. It would have worried Ludovic if I had had to leave the estate at this particular time, there is so much to be seen to before we ...' A faint blush stained her face. 'Oh, but I mustn't say. Not until Ludovic agrees I may. Perhaps this evening. He is being very mysterious about dinner tonight. I shouldn't be surprised if . . .' She broke off with an artificial laugh. 'But there, you're being too persuasive, my dear. I had no intention whatsoever of saying so much. But now, truly I must go, or Ludovic will never forgive me.' She jumped up and with a wave of one small hand left Krista to her own thoughts.

And shortly afterwards they could be seen, Ludovic and the Comtesse, strolling down the steps leading to the rose garden, then slowly along a path which led to the woods. As usual her hand was through his arm, she was looking up into his face and he was smiling down, his eyes filled with adoration. She couldn't see that particular detail, of course. But it was firmly fixed in her mind. Driving her mad.

It would have been ridiculous to refuse Philippe's invitation. She told herself so as they drove along the winding roads leading from the château. Nothing on earth would have persuaded her to stay in a situation where she might have been asked to drink a toast to the happy pair. And what did it matter if he thought her devious? She had as much as told him she would refuse Philippe's invitation, but there was no reason why she shouldn't change her mind. Her free time was her own. She had spent all the day hanging about the château, trying to fill in time while he had been off heaven knew where. He had said he wanted to look up an old friend, had asked if she would like to be dropped off in Morlaix, but had been perfectly understanding when she had refused.

'Yes, you do look a bit tired, *drágám*.' There had been a whisper of mischief in the dark eyes which assessed her with such penetration. 'It must be all these sleepless nights.'

But before her heart could warm to him, even by
a few degrees, Barbe had appeard at his elbow, her
manner as cool to the girl as it was warm to him.
'Are you ready, Ludovic?' She spoke in French,
which caused him to raise an eyebrow before
replying pointedly in English.

'Quite ready. I have been trying to persuade
Krista to come along for the drive.'

'I'm sorry, Krista.' Swiftly she apologised for
the lapse. 'I keep forgetting that you don't speak
French.'

'Don't apologise, Comtesse. Besides, that much
even I can understand.'

'Well, of course you did.' Her tone said that
only an idiot would have misunderstood. 'I'm
sorry you won't come. But you must have a rest,
and ask for tea whenever you want it.'

They had been late in returning to the château,
so late that Krista had been almost ready for her
date before she saw that the car had returned to its
normal position on the wide circle of gravel in
front of the house. But that suited her, because she
was able to make her escape, leaving a brief note
with Hortense which explained her movements.

She did not enjoy her evening with Philippe.
And that served her right, she decided. All the
friendly sparkle which had brightened her on the
first time seemed to have evaporated, and she
found him dull and abstracted. Trying to be
honest, she had to admit that she possibly wasn't
the best of company, and he too was probably
regretting whatever impulse had led him to make
the suggestion the previous evening. No sooner
had the question come into her mind than she was
expressing it.

'Did the Comtesse suggest you should ask me
out this evening, Philippe?'

'The Comtesse?' He grimaced, narrowing his eyes as if he had been asked to solve an impossible riddle. 'What a strange question!' He lifted the cigarette which had smouldered irritatingly in the ashtray since they had arrived at the restaurant. 'Of course not,' he said belatedly. 'Why should you think such a thing?' As if realising how far short he had fallen as host he leaned across the table towards her, eyes narrowing to assure her of his genuine interest, his reason for asking her out.

'Perhaps,' regretting his change of manner—the original had suited her perfectly—Krista leaned back in her seat, out of reach should he be inclined to try some hand-holding. 'Perhaps Philippe because of the way we met the other night. The more I think of it the more it seems an unlikely coincidence.'

He was taken aback. She could see that, but a split second later he laughed and looked down at his plate rather sheepishly. 'Well, maybe you are right, *chérie*. Only——' the black lustrous eyes returned to her face, dwelt lovingly on hair and mouth before looking directly, appealingly into hers, 'only I did not mean you to know that.' He shrugged. 'It is not the thing a man always chooses to tell, especially not to the woman concerned. I came here deliberately the other evening because I knew you would be here.'

'You knew?' Krista disregarded his blandishing manner. 'Who told you?'

'Well,' he smiled apologetically, 'it was the merest chance. But a happy chance, a piece of luck for me. You see, I heard Barbe mention to Jean-Paul that you would be staying at the Cheval Blanc that evening and . . .'

Humiliation that everyone seemed to know of her summary dismissal from the château made her

skin burn but she interrupted him with a
semblance of coolness. '. . . And you decided you
would have to see me again, come what may.'

'Now you are laughing at me.'

'No, I'm quite serious. I don't usually have that
effect on men.'

'Then they must all be mad, or blind—or both.'

Sensing that she would be given no further
information on the subject, Krista abandoned it
and began to speak instead about some less
personal matter, and she was not surprised when
she saw an expression of relief on her companion's face. From that she was able to draw
her own conclusions. Whatever the reason for
Philippe's persistence she was positive it was not
the one he had given her. Even now he gave no
sign of being in the company of a woman he
found irresistible. While they talked idly, her
mind raced round the problem till she was giddy.
And the only conclusion she could reach was
that perhaps Barbe had felt guilty about her
behaviour and had asked him to take pity on the
unwelcome guest.

It was late when they left the restaurant, very
much later than Krista had thought. And yet when
Philippe suggested that they drive back to the
château via the coast road she could not object. It
was such a beautiful night, with a full moon
bathing the earth in a silvery light that it seemed a
pity to hurry indoors. Besides, the longer she
waited the less chance there was of bumping into
Barbe or Ludovic, and as the front door was never
locked there would be no question of finding
herself shut out.

When they reached a spot high on a cliff
overlooking the sea, Philippe drew the car on to
the roadside and they sat for a while, each deep in

thought, he smoking with that dedicated intensity which afflicts so many Frenchmen. Once he put an arm about her shoulders in an attempt to draw her close to him, but when she resisted he seemed to realise how pointless it was.

'Perhaps we'd better go back, Philippe.' She peered at the tiny face of her watch, surprised to see that it was almost two o'clock. 'I'm feeling really sleepy now.' To underline the fact she yawned, then smothered it with a hand and an apology. 'Forgive me—but I haven't been sleeping very well.'

'Of course.' He started the engine, showing no sign of the pique which would have been the natural response of a man who was emotionally involved.

But when they reached the château and stopped on the wide sweep of gravel he seemed to have quite different inclinations. Instead of the formal but friendly goodnight which Krista quite expected she found herself locked in his arms while he gazed down at her with every indication of besotted passion. She was so startled she looked up at him in the way she might have done had she been offering her lips.

When he kissed her she adopted the tactics which had been so effective with Iain, of remaining totally quiescent until her lack of response could not fail to be noticed.

'Bonsoir, chérie.' His voice was low, as if he was determined to act the romantic.

'Bonsoir.' Coldly she tried to disengage herself, furious with him for forcing them both to endure this farcical behaviour, even more furious with herself for getting into this embarrassing situation.

'Chérie!' His arms released her, but he stroked his fingers down her cheek in a lingering last farewell, quite the impatient lover saying a reluctant goodnight. Almost a convincing act!

Angrily Krista stalked away from him, feet in thin shoes crunching uncomfortably over the gravel. She sensed that Philippe was still there watching her as she fumbled with the heavy metal clasp but as she pushed open the door the engine fired, lights swept round in an arc, then accelerated down the drive. She sighed wearily as she closed the door, standing a moment in the stillness. Now it was hard to understand just why she had chosen to go out with Philippe. It would have been so much more sensible to have had an early night.

Hardly thinking what she was doing, she removed her shoes, holding them by their slender straps and walking across the cool marble tiling of the hall. Shafts of moonlight struck through the windows illuminating corners, and as she reached the foot of the curving staircase somewhere to her right there was the sound of a light switch and there standing in the archway of the corridor stood Ludovic, looking angrier than she had ever seen him before.

It was a long time before either of them spoke. Or maybe it just seemed so. In any case, Krista was trembling so much from shock and taut nerves she would scarcely have had the strength to speak.

'Where the hell do you think you have been?' He ground out the words in a strange accent, at once forbidding and sensuous.

'I . . . I . . .' She had forgotten the shoes she was holding in her hands, but all at once he seemed larger, more menacing than she remembered. Then a trickle of courage, of defiance, returned to her veins. 'I thought you would know where I had been. Didn't Barbe tell you?' She asked the question rather pertly.

'Come into the study,' he said curtly. 'I don't propose to stand here rowing with you.'

For a moment she looked at his back, her instincts telling her to run upstairs, to have the showdown with him at a time of her choosing, not his. Any time but now, in fact, but before she could decide to race up the long winding stairs he turned back to her with a frown of impatience, so she had no choice in the matter.

'Well?' When the door had been firmly closed behind her he stood, hands on hips, that same domineering angry expression on his face. His eyes she saw were cold as ice floes and seemed to bore into her skull. 'I'm waiting.'

'Waiting for Godot?' She tried to sound casual, provocative, but her legs unexpectedly weakened and she sank into the nearest chair, quite spoiling the effect, remembered her shoes and struggled to pull them on to her feet. A whit more confident now, she looked up again at the angry face. 'You said you were waiting, Ludovic?'

'I want to know where you've been. I shan't ask again,' he said with barely controlled impatience.

'We were at the . . .' she racked her brain in a pretence at remembering, 'Ah yes, the Auberge Napoléon. It's in a village called . . .'

'I know what the village is called.' He spoke in a tone of suppressed fury.

'I must say you're being extremely unreasonable. You demand to know where I've been, and when I tell you it only makes you more angry.'

'It's half-past one. You don't mean to tell me you've been in the Napoléon till this time?'

'No.' Resenting the advantage his height gave him, Krista got to her feet. 'No, I shan't tell you that. Especially as you seem so determined to find fault with anything I'm likely to say.'

'So,' he spoke through gritted teeth, 'just where have you been?'

'Oh, we've been looking at the moonlight on the water.' She waved a casual arm while carefully avoiding his eyes. 'You know how it is when people go out on a date.'

'Yes, I know how it is.' He took her arm in an iron grasp and swung her round towards him, forcing her chin up so that it was impossible to play at avoiding his eyes. 'I know exactly how it is with people like Philippe Duclos. And that's why I'm determined to find out what happened between you tonight.'

'What on earth do you think happened?' It was a struggle to keep back the tears. 'And if you don't mind, you're hurting me. At least Philippe didn't do that!'

He released her so abruptly she almost fell, but now, far from wishing to avoid him, she glared at him with antagonism. 'Besides,' she didn't quite wish him to make any mistakes on the subject 'we're friends that's all. Just friends,' she added ridiculously.

'So that is why,' his anger seemed now to have been replaced by scorn, a much more hurtful emotion, 'you told me you were not going out with him this evening. Strange, when you are such friends. And because you are just friends you indulged in that tender scene out there on the drive—without regard to anyone who might be watching.'

Krista felt her skin burn and stifled the sob that rose to her lips. 'I shouldn't have thought anyone would have watched—not anyone with any self-respect. It's not the kind of thing that decent people watch.'

'No?' He gave a slight laugh while his eyes

continued to look bleakly at her. 'It seems to me I had little choice in the matter. I heard the car, it seemed natural to go to the window to see if you had come back safely.' He took a cheroot from the pocket of his jacket and flicked a lighter. 'Do you consider I have no right to be concerned about your welfare? While you are with me, away from your home and family, then I am very much concerned with the kind of people you mix with.'

'Has it occurred to you,' now she was speaking very coldly, showing how much she resented his interference in her affairs, 'that I'm twenty-three, nearly twenty-four, and long past the age when most girls have branched out on their own? I don't need a keeper, thank you very much!'

'You may think you do not, but according to my way of looking at things you do. And I do not like to think of you being out with Philippe Duclos till the early hours of the morning.'

'I wish you would tell me why you consider him such an unsuitable companion. You keep going on about that—it's most aggravating. I suppose it's pointless to tell you that he behaved perfectly well when he was with me.'

'If you say so then I must believe you.'

'You need not sound so reluctant, as if you would much rather think the worst of me.'

'Not of you—of him.'

'Oh, for heaven's sake!' In exasperation Krista turned away from him. 'He's a great friend of your . . .' The word fiancée hovered on her lips, but she was reluctant to speak it, feeling that once admitted between them then Barbe's position in his life would be fully acknowledged. '. . . One of your best friends.'

'That may be. But one cannot always like the

friends of one's friends. Besides, Jean-Paul sometimes lacks discretion.'

She was surprised that he had decided she meant
Jean-Paul rather than his sister, surprised but
relieved by a postponement however short.
'Anyway,' it was unusual for her to be so
determined but on this occasion she meant to have
the last word, 'I still can't see what the fuss is
about. I'm quite sure that you and Barbe did not
spend the evening yearning for my company.'

'You think not?' He spoke without removing the
cheroot from his strong white teeth.

'I'm sure of it,' she scoffed, then wondered why,
when she was so anxious to forget her she had
reintroduced that name.

'I cannot speak for Barbe, only for myself.'

'You surprise me.'

'And what . . .' Ludovic took the cigar from his
lips and held it for a moment before grinding it
out in a ferocious little gesture in a large china dish
which resided on the desk. '. . . what do you mean
by that?'

'I mean,' she smiled in what she knew was
bound to be a very aggravating kind of way, 'I
mean exactly what you meant when you were
criticising me for going out with Philippe. What's
sauce for the goose, you know.'

'What's sauce for the goose,' the words were
almost snarled at her while he grabbed her again
by the shoulders, fingers biting cruelly into the soft
flesh of her upper arm, 'is not necessarily sauce for
the gander. At least,' he spat, 'not for this gander!'
The blue eyes flashed with anger, contempt,
despair, one of these or all. And the feelings, the
soft seductive feelings which his touch, even this
ungentle savage touch, caused to lick and flicker
through her veins made her long to put her head

on his breast and weep. Instead she returned stare for stare, ignoring all her feminine weakness.

But then he spoke again, this time less the brutal inquisitor, more the man who, with a flick of a finger, the raising of an eyebrow could exert his will over her. 'Why are we arguing, Krista? *Drágám!*' The endearment brought an easing of the pain about her chest, all the biting animosity she felt for him started to slip away. His fingers lost their unkind strength, shook her a little in affectionate amusement and his lips curved into a smile. Another tiny shake. 'Can you tell me?'

'I wasn't arguing.' Her grey eyes were soft with longing as she looked up at him. If only, if only he would put his arms about her and pull her close to him!

'Of course you weren't. I was the one who was arguing. You must forgive me. Since you came into my life I have become like a hen with one chick.' He released her with another little shake and leaned back against the desk. 'All these farmyard images!'

'May I go to bed now?' All emotion had been drained from her in that little gesture of rejection. That and the implication they were of different generations. Ludovic looked on her as a child.

'You see, Krista?' maybe he had caught from her expression some clue as to her feelings, 'I feel responsible for you—taking you away from your aunt.'

'Yes, I've often wondered about that.' She turned to the door. 'I still can't understand why you did.'

'Can't you, Krista?' He was still smiling as he caught her again, turned her round to face him. 'I thought you knew. It was to allow you to escape, to stretch your wings, to get away from all the

limitations, the slavery imposed on you by
Traquhair Lodge and Lady James.'

'And instead,' when she began speaking she
meant her words to be a lighthearted remark, a
teasing little comment but that was not how they
came out. Even in her own ears they were sour
with resentment, abrasive and mean, 'I merely
exchanged one form of slavery for another.'

A film of shock clouded his eyes, a disbelieving
look making them first widen, then narrow in one
of the cold angers to which he was occasionally
subject.

'You do not mean that, Krista.' Still his voice
was soft, seductive as if he was uncertain that he
had really heard the words, as if he were willing
her to deny them.

And she longed to respond, to laugh, to say that
of course she had been joking; she even imagined
herself linking her arms about his neck and
brushing her lips against his in a continuation of
the teasing. But that was the last thing she could
afford to do, that could betray totally just how
deeply she felt for him.

'Of course I mean it.' There was a shade of
conciliation in her voice, but Ludovic did not hear
it.

'So!' With the narrowed eyes, the dark skin, the
words issuing through lips that scarcely parted, he
seemed the epitome of all that was strange and
menacing. Krista drew in a short breath, gazed up
at him with fear as well as some perverse
fascination. 'So that is what you think of me!'
Abruptly his fingers released her. He gave the
impression of distaste, almost rubbing his hands
down the sides of his dark slacks.

'I think you have a very convenient attitude to
these things.' It was hard to continue in her brisk,

brittle way when she was longing to throw herself against him, longing to be held to his chest, to hear his heart beating close to her ear. But that was impossible, so she went on, 'I came away with you simply to help you out. I was perfectly happy in Edinburgh and my first reaction to your suggestion, if you can remember it . . .'

'I remember,' he interrupted very coolly.

In spite of her self-imposed calm she could not control the faint colour in her cheeks. 'It was only when I decided it was my duty that I gave in to my aunt's persuasions.'

'Thank you. I'm glad you explained properly.' He looked at her without expression. 'I'm sorry it has been such a chore for you. I had not meant it to be like that. My only excuse is that as I find it all so stimulating I expect other people to have similar reactions. Then,' turning away from her, he raked long fingers through his hair, 'it is as well that we are so close to the return to Edinburgh, and of course I do not expect you to consider coming to the States with me. I would not think of imposing on you any longer than is necessary.'

'Very well.' It was absurd to feel so hurt, so rejected, when her own words had precipitated them both into this harsh unforgiving mood. 'Then if I'm allowed to go to bed now . . .' She walked past him towards the door, pausing with her hand on the knob.

Anger smouldered in the dark eyes which looked at her with such dislike, but before he answered he came towards her with that lithe soft tread which so often reminded her of a jungle cat. Then they stood together, so close that Krista felt his breath on her face, and she was very conscious of her heart hammering painfully against her ribs.

'You do not need my permission to go to bed,

Krista.' With his face half in shadow there was a
brooding menace in him, his voice had lost all its
light cadence, the foreign accent deepened. 'You
are a free agent. As you have just reminded me,
you are no longer a child. Perhaps that is where I
have gone wrong, trying to ignore . . .' His voice
drifted away before he could explain exactly what
he meant. Or perhaps it had never been his
intention to do that.

Before she knew what he was about he had
reached out, pulling her against him, gazing down
into her face with a dominating expression. Krista
knew a moment's softening, she prepared to
respond when his mouth sought hers, gave way to
the familiar licking fire that his touch inevitably
inspired.

But the mouth that could be so gentle, so
persuasive had abandoned tenderness and sought
now only to subdue and demean. For a moment
the pleasure lasted before she tore herself away
from him, thrust him aside and stood, breast
heaving, eyes flashing in the subdued lighting.

'There you are, *kedvenc*,' his voice was taunting,
coldly patronising, 'you may go now. But,' one dark
hand was placed flat against the door as she whirled
away from him, 'think about what you said. If you
were my slave I would be unlikely to stop there.
Always assuming that I wanted to go further, of
course.' The bar to her exit was removed with a
contemptuous little shrug. 'And we both know that
would be ridiculous. Go to bed, Krista. You have
my permission. And sleep well.'

The cruel edge to his laughter followed her all
the way along the corridor, up the stairs and into
her bedroom. It was only when she threw herself
on to the bed that she finally understood the
sound was in her head.

CHAPTER EIGHT

KRISTA was glad that Ludovic had gone before she went down the following morning, because she did not know how she was to be able to face him. The night had given her time to consider her behaviour, the foolish words she had thrown at him in the altercation they had in the early hours of the morning.

Now the thought could only make her burn with embarrassment. It was unlike her to react so impetuously. She would not have believed that love could be such a painful, destructive emotion. But of course it wasn't only love which had caused the reaction, it was jealousy, sheer blinding jealousy, something she had never experienced before and with which she was unable to deal.

If only it had not been Barbe! If it had been a woman she could like or respect, then, she told herself, she would have been able to accept an engagement, could have faced the fact that Ludovic loved someone else, that he was not the man she had all her life been dreaming of.

She sipped the scalding coffee and gave a faint groan. Why should she trouble to deceive herself? It wouldn't matter who he was going to marry, she would feel the same torture, the same tearing pain when she thought of him holding another woman in his arms. And it was surprising just how often, in spite of her determination to exclude them, such pictures kept invading her mind. Barbe being held, smiling up into his face . . .

As if on cue the door of the small breakfast

room opened and Barbe stood there, looking immaculate in a tailored linen dress, black with tan trim round the neckline and banding the short sleeves. She was smiling, but there was a careful expression in her black eyes as they surveyed her visitor's face, doubtless noticing the increasing shadowy unhappiness on the younger girl's face.

'*Bonjour, chérie.* You slept well?'

'Yes,' Krista lied, looking deeply into her cup. 'Very well.'

'Hmm,' said Barbe assessingly. 'You were late.' There was the merest shade of censure in her manner. 'Ludovic was concerned.'

'He had no need to be.' Still refusing to look at her hostess, Krista pushed back her chair. 'I suppose I'd better go along and check on the arrangements. I'd . . .'

'Oh, he asked me to tell you that he would not need you today.' Her voice was sharp with suppressed emotions. 'Somehow I got the distinct impression that you and he were . . . not on the best of terms with each other.'

'Really?' Krista paused with one hand on the door handle, but she could not resist waiting, torturing herself to hear whatever else the Frenchwoman had to say to her. For there was the firm impression that she had by no means finished.

'Yes. It is so silly, these little misunderstandings, and I'm hoping it will not continue for too long. You see,' there was the sound of coffee pouring into a cup, then of a spoon stirring sugar, 'I feel strongly about it. Our evening, the one which should have been so . . . memorable, was quite ruined.'

Slowly Krista swung round to look at her. There had been an edge in the voice hinting at disappointment, more than disappointment, barely concealed fury, perhaps. She stared at the bland features of the woman sitting at the table, bland till you looked at the eyes and saw the anger lurking there.

'And quite frankly, Miss Ewing,' quite suddenly the guise of concern was dropped, words like *chérie* or even her Christian name were abandoned, at least while they were alone together, 'I find it tedious always to have a third person hanging about. Why should Ludovic be worried about you and your paltry little affairs? Surely he employs you to save him from worry, not to be its cause.'

Krista felt the colour drain from her face as she stared into the features of the Comtesse. She had a longing to put her hands over her ears and to run from the room, and was stopped only by the firm suspicion that such behaviour would have pleased the Comtesse enormously.

'Ludovic has no need to feel himself responsible for me. I'm quite capable of looking after myself.'

Barbe's laugh was shrill, a hint of hysteria lurking in its depths. 'Of course you can. I told Ludovic so last night. You are not a child, but he persists in regarding you as one. You must have been very clever to encourage such a protective attitude in him, so that when you go out with a young man he grows quite anxious when you have not come home by midnight.'

'There was no need for him to worry.' In spite of her agitated pulses Krista was keeping a firm hold on herself. 'After all, I was with one of your best friends, wasn't I?'

The words uttered in such innocence had a strange effect on Barbe, who drew in a hissing breath, her eyes glittered brilliantly as she got to her feet and came across the room to the door. Krista looked with a kind of fascinated horror, unaware of what she had said to incense the other woman to this extent.

'And what . . . what exactly do you mean by that?'

'By—by what?' She grasped the handle more firmly, gaining some sort of confidence from the smooth feel of worn brass under her fingers. 'I didn't mean anything. I understood Philippe Duclos was one of your friends. And,' she realised that Barbe had offered her a weapon which she would be a fool to ignore, 'it seems strange that Ludovic hates it so much when I go out with a friend of the family.'

Before she had time to understand what was happening she saw Barbe's hand flash in front of her, felt the sting, heard the slap as the small fingers struck at her cheek. Tears, of shock, of humiliation, stood in her eyes, but she refused to allow them to fall. Instead she surveyed the Comtesse with all the self-possession she could muster, speaking in a quiet voice behind which her real feelings were concealed.

'If you'll excuse me, I'll go to the study. I have no intention of becoming involved in a brawl like a . . . like a fishwife!' She pulled the door, but Barbe prevented it opening properly.

'Yes, go!' There was a world of contempt in the older woman's dismissal. 'Go, Miss Ewing! If you are wise you will go—for good. You are a handicap to Ludovic instead of the help that you are supposed to be.' She laughed, shortly, without humour. 'His trouble is that he has always been too kindhearted, picking up waifs and strays along the way.'

There was a long fraught silence while the full import of the words dripped slowly, bleakly into Krista's consciousness. Then without her willing it she heard her own voice. 'Is that what he said?'

'Oh, not in so many words. He wouldn't, would he? Not Ludovic. Only I was able to piece the story together—about how he felt sorry for you, with this aunt. He thought it would be good, kind, if he could help you to escape. That is all he wanted, not to have his kindness taken advantage of.'

'Thank you, Comtesse. It must be very satisfying for you to speak as you have. But of course I can't accept all you've told me. I'm employed by Ludovic, not by you. When he wants me to leave, then of course I shall. But until then . . .' Fighting the tears which were tying knots in her chest, Krista tried to pull the door wider.

'But don't you see, that is something he will find hard to do. No matter what he feels, he will be most reluctant to ask you to go. He will struggle on hoping that perhaps you will take the initiative, that you will see he no longer can make excuses for your presence. If I were you . . .' Barbe paused so long that in spite of herself Krista felt her attention pulled back to that strikingly beautiful face. Beautiful except for the hardness of the eyes, the narrow line of the mouth.

'What I would do if I were you . . .' Now that she had the other girl's full attention Barbe continued, giving the impression that she was offering a deeply considered opinion. '. . . I would not risk the humiliation of being asked to go. I would make some excuse and tell him you must return to Edinburgh. He knows you have a young man there. Perhaps you could tell him . . .'

'No!' In spite of her earlier words Krista had an almost overwhelming urge to wipe the faint smirk from the other woman's face. But it was an urge which she knew she must control. 'No, I shan't take your advice, Comtesse. If I decide to go home

then I shall think of my own lies. I don't need
yours.'

At last the door gave way and she was able to
escape from the room, to walk along the corridor,
head high, still struggling with the effort to stop
the tears streaming down her cheeks. When she
reached the small study, she lay for a few moments
against the closed door, eyes closed, aware only of
the pain that was racking her body.

He had told Barbe so much about her—that was
the thought causing the most lacerating pain.
Ludovic had confided in Barbe, telling her of the
circumstances of Krista's life in Edinburgh.
Perhaps he had even told her of Iain's overheard
words in the garden of Traquhair Lodge, they
might have laughed together at it, he could have
confessed that while it had been amusing for a
little while to have such an obviously lovesick girl
at his elbow, it had palled very quickly.

She opened her eyes, seeing the room, the desk,
and was at once taken back to the previous
evening, to the blazing row they had had right
here, on this very spot. And it was then the most
wounding idea of all came into her mind, refusing
to be removed. He must have asked Barbe to drop
a few hints, to make sure that she got the message.
Anything to spare him the embarrassment of
telling her her services were no longer required.
And to save her as well, she thought numbly. It
was true enough what Barbe had said, he was
kind. And he would hate to humiliate her. So there
was only one thing she could do: she had to make
it easy for him. At least she owed him that.

But when she met him late that afternoon, when
with Barbe they came together for some tea,
Krista found that she almost lost her resolve. His
eyes, the one that had flashed in anger the

previous night, had now assumed all that faintly
mocking amusement against which she had no
defence. Barbe too was amiable, quite as if there
had been no wild exchange of words early that
day, as if the physical attack on her guest was
merely an aberrant dream. She fulfilled totally the
role of perfect hostess, thus it was impossible to
avoid concluding that she was the ideal wife for a
world-famous conductor.

'You have an easy day, *drágám*?'

Only Krista saw the flash of animosity in
Barbe's eyes at the term of endearment, but it was
quickly veiled as she returned her attention to the
silver teapot.

'Yes.' Of course he had no idea that she had
spent the day driving about the country, making
arrangements for a hurried return to her own
country. 'Very easy.'

'Good.' Her reply seemed to satisfy him and
over the rim of his cup the dark eyes were
conciliatory, as if he were apologising to her,
willing her to accept his milder mood. 'You have
been looking a little tired. If I've been overworking
you then I apologise.' His eyes flicked away and he
smiled at their hostess. 'If Barbe had not told me
then heaven knows when I would have noticed.'

'Like all men you are very self-obsessed.' It was
so unlike Barbe to make anything that vaguely
resembled a joke that Krista blinked in surprise.

'I'll try to remember that.' He grinned at the
two women. 'But I shan't promise. I . . .' He broke
off when the door opened and the maid told her
mistress that someone wished to speak to her on
the telephone. After a few moments' interrogation
Barbe got up in something of a huff and walked
with short quick steps from the room, leaving the
door conspicuously open behind her. There was a

brief silence during which Krista became aware of her heart pulsating in agitation and she struggled to keep her eyes averted from the one place in the room she longed to look.

'Krista.' All the throbbing magic, the sensuous delight she had dreamed of was in that single word, the struggle was over, and she looked up into Ludovic's eyes. Their depth of colour struck her as it had done that first time, the intensity of the dark blue, the brilliance of the white seeming to tell everything about the man. 'Krista.' He repeated her name, rolling the consonants as if he were gaining as much pleasure from the sound as he was giving. 'You slept well last night, *drágám*?'

'No.' She had meant to say yes, but the lie wouldn't come. Not when he was looking at her with that particularly seductive way. 'No, I hardly slept at all.'

'And you blame me?'

'No, of course not. Why should I blame you?'

'Perhaps because our row was my fault. I should not have questioned you as I did. You were quite right, *drágám*—what you do in your spare time is none of my business. You are a free agent and quite capable of making your own decisions. If you choose to go out with Philippe Duclos then you must do so.' He waited, but there was no reply and his expression altered slightly.

But I didn't, Krista mourned silently. I didn't choose to go out with him. I only agreed because I was jealous, jealous that you'd gone off for the day with Barbe. And I wanted to pay you back. But of course she could say none of these things, and before she could think of some words that would satisfy the occasion he went on.

'You are coming to tonight's concert, *chérie*?'

'No.' A brief shake of her head. It was

impossible for her to say that Barbe had almost forbidden her to come.

'I see.' He sighed. 'Well, there is no need if you do not want to come. But I have planned to take you to dinner afterwards—you and Barbe as a special celebration, and . . .'

But before he could complete what he had been going to say Barbe came back into the room, protesting loudly about the man who had kept her chatting on the telephone for so long but looking suspiciously from Krista to Ludovic. Then, seeming relieved to find them still occupying their original seats, she sat down and began to discuss her telephone call.

Under cover of their conversation Krista took the opportunity to run upstairs to her room, desperate to escape the evidence of her own eyes and ears. Until now, deep down she had not totally believed what Barbe had told her. She couldn't, *couldn't* believe that Ludovic was in love with Barbe, that he meant to marry her. But what other purpose could there be for the dinner party, this special celebration, the celebration which had been postponed from the previous evening? Now she had little doubt that the engagement would be announced, after the successful completion of his programme in Brittany, a programme surely planned only to please the woman he loved.

But she was not given time to torture herself with these thoughts, for only moments later there was a knock at the door, a knock so firm and confident that she was not surprised when the door opened and Ludovic came into the room.

'You did not answer my question, Krista.' Much of the gentleness he had shown downstairs seemed to have disappeared, and she was reminded forcefully of the anger he had shown the previous night when they had thrown those bitter accusations at each other.

'Your question?' She knew well enough what he meant, but the procrastination gave her a little time to regain some of her self-control.

'Question.' He shook his head in irritation at the same time raking his fingers through his hair. She watched it fall over his forehead, wondered at the faintly distracted look in his eyes, strange in a man as assured of himself as Ludovic Hasek. 'At least it was intended as a question. You will, I hope, join us for dinner this evening.'

Krista hesitated deliberately before she rejected it, unwilling for him to know that she had made up her mind much earlier. 'I don't think I will, thank you. As I told you, I didn't sleep well last night,' or the previous ones, her eyes silently reminded him, 'and I hardly think I'll be able to keep my eyes open.'

'I see.' His mouth, the one that could be so tender, so seductive was a hard thin line. 'And what if I ask you to come, Krista? If I suggest that you owe it to me as your employer, that you owe it to Barbe as your hostess to come tonight?'

It was that conjunction of their names which dismissed a lingering inclination for her to change her mind, which underlined, reminded her of the reasons why she dared not go. And so that he would not continue with his persuasions she returned to their row of the previous night.

'I thought,' the gibe was as cruel to herself as it was to him, but she pretended satisfaction at the way his eyes darkened at her words, 'I thought we had agreed you were not to interfere in my private life. It's one thing to be at your beck and call all day long, but I do think I'm entitled to *some* time to myself.'

'So ...' He took a step towards her, so menacing that she moved away from him, finding herself trapped against the large bed, her hand clinging to the corner post for support. 'So, those things you said to me last night were not impetuous words thrown in the heat of the moment.'

'Oh,' she tried to inject a note of amusement into her voice, saw by his narrowed eyes how successful she had been, 'I wish I hadn't said them. But now I have there seems little point in denying them. They may even have cleared the air a bit.' The hardboiled sound of her voice stunned her momentarily.

Ludovic said a word, one she had never heard before, but from the venom in his voice she guessed was far from complimentary and at the same time his hands reached out for her shoulders. Their touch was a reflection of his feelings, hard and cruel, and he seemed to find satisfaction in the way he shook her.

Unable to keep her balance with the side of the bed pressing against her legs, Krista fell back on to it, looking up half dismayed, half excited by the expression on his face. For a moment he bent over her, fury reflected in his eyes, then his fingers twisted in the disordered coils of her hair, spread about the old gold of the antique bedspread, and he lowered his body to join hers.

If she had expected a repetition of that brief idyllic interlude on the beach the first few seconds of his embrace were enough to disabuse her. Then, his mouth on hers had been tender, beguiling, evoking a trembling response, a slow combustion in vein and artery, but now his mouth took hers in anger, tenderness was renounced as his arms sought to strain her body ever more closely to his, as if determined to make her aware of every inch of that powerful frame.

It was a kiss, an embrace she should have loathed, would have hated if it had originated in any other man. Instead she revelled in the intimate exploration of her body, her senses were intoxicated by his touch and the thin material of her dress ceased to exist. She moaned as his mouth moved to her eyes, to her throat, its path burning a trail across the softness of her skin, willing for just a few moments to allow her body to respond to the urgent onslaught.

And then, just at the very last second, while she felt herself being overwhelmed, being rushed to the precipice of her own emotions, she dragged her mouth away from his, pushed with all her strength at the hard wall of his chest, at the same time rolling away from him on the wide soft bed. For a long time she lay listening to the sound of her own breathing, gasping, choking, then she turned her face so that she was looking directly into his eyes, so close to her own.

'How dare you!' She forced the sob from her voice, made herself sound genuinely outraged, conveniently forgetting how a moment earlier she had exulted in the possessive domination of his mouth. 'How dare you behave like that!'

He did not reply, but lay there, looking at her, eyes dark, mysterious, revealing nothing of his feelings. Only the pulse in one cheek, the tightly controlled set of his mouth might have given her some clue to his deepest emotions. But she was too overwrought, too anxious to hide her own tattered weariness to have much concern for his feelings.

'Come, Krista.' With a lazy move he got up from the bed and stood looking at her with the same inscrutable expression. 'Don't be quite so naïve. It doesn't take courage for a man to kiss a girl. I told you that once before, did I not?' He paused, eyes searching her face as if willing her to remember, to make some response. 'Kissing is for pleasure, for mutual comfort between a man and a woman. So,' her lack of response caused his eyes to narrow again, 'when you ask how I dare, I say I only did what seemed natural, instinctive.'

Not that he wanted to! Not that she looked so beautiful he could not resist her! Just that it was natural—instinctive! Human nature after all! Pain threatened to overwhelm her.

'And yet,' her voice was brittle, affected, 'at the very suggestion that other people might be responding to what was natural, instinctive, you seem to lose your cool.'

'We're back to Philippe Duclos again.' This time there was no mistaking the contempt in his voice nor the flash of disdain in his eyes. 'Obviously what I said about him is not going to be so easily forgotten. Well, I take it all back.'

'At least he didn't kiss me in that totally disgusting way!' She rose from the bed and looked at him, eyes flashing, bosom heaving, feeling a flare of satisfaction in the angry darkening of his face. She expected him to throw the words back in her face, but when he spoke it was with a control that was more insulting than a blatant show of anger would have been.

'Well, there's no accounting for tastes. And if Duclos is yours then there's nothing more to be said. Only,' his eyes raked her from the top of her dishevelled head to her unshod feet, 'don't expect me to admire you for it.' A second later the door of the bedroom closed behind him.

Krista stared at it for a long time, seeing with absolute clarity each grain of the finely polished

wood, each knot and imperfection of the intricate
marbling, and yet seeing nothing. Despair filled
her, tore at her, the tears she could not shed lay
like a stone in her chest.

She would never learn. Ludovic had been
right—she was naïve. Especially when it came to
dealing with men. She had had the opportunity to
study him over the months, knew what made him
tick, as much as anyone would ever know about
him. And yet she had handled the occasion so
badly. He had wanted to make love to her: little as
she knew about such things that much had been
insistently clear. And yet, given the opportunity,
one that she knew would never be repeated, she
had thrown it back in his face. With an insult
added to make sure he got the message, to make
sure that her virginity would never be so offended
again.

Slowly, without really understanding what she
was about, Krista turned and walked over to the
cheval glass which stood in the corner of the bedroom between the window and the door of the
bathroom. At first she could hardly recognise the
face which had been so familiar for twenty-five
years. She was slimmer than she had been. In spite
of all the food, the rich dishes, the specialities in
every country in Europe, she seemed in the last
day or two to have lost an inch or so from her
waist. That made her look taller, even minus the
high heels abandoned when Ludovic had pushed
her back on to the bed. The thought of it made her
face grow warm, brought a glitter to her eyes as
she relived those moments, trying to wipe out the
ending, to substitute another that would have been
far more to her liking.

Even to think of it made a slow fire start deep
inside her, flaring with sudden ferocity to consume

her with the pain of unsatisfied longings. At last the easing tears began to pour down her cheeks and she ran over to throw herself on to the bed, where she lay with her face pressed on the indentation caused by his head. Mingling with the smell of the bedcover her nostrils caught the subtle unusual scent of his cologne, and she forced her head still deeper in a desperate attempt to absorb the lingering proof of his presence. But her tears seemed to quench it and all her fevered passionate repetition of his name could not restore the living man to her. Her influence in his life was as evanescent, as ephemeral as the scent on the cover. She had to face the fact that both had gone as if they had never existed.

CHAPTER NINE

IT was strange to leave the château in the early hours of the morning, almost as if she were doing a flit without paying the rent. The idea came to her mind as she sat stony-eyed behind the chauffeur as he drove her to the nearest station.

'There is an early train for Paris,' Barbe had told her when she had been making her plans the previous night. 'Then you can be home before it is too late.'

And Krista had allowed herself to be persuaded—foolishly perhaps. It was a bleak admission, one that came much too late. It would be too ridiculous if she were to rap on the glass partition that separated her from the driver and tell him to go back the way they had come. That way, she glanced at the face of her watch, she would reach the château just as Ludovic would be coming down for breakfast. Or maybe, the thought strengthened her resolve, maybe they would be breakfasting together in Barbe's room. As they had done before.

She had heard no sound of their return last night, even though she had lain awake listening for them. Had they come tiptoeing up the long winding staircase, she wondered, holding hands and laughing silently in their efforts to disturb no one? Once during the long hours which had ticked away with infinite slowness Krista had had the wild idea that she would go down and wait for them. She would skulk in the passage and startle them by switching on the lights in parody of Ludovic's actions when she had stayed out late.

How would he have liked it, she asked the question tearfully, if she had behaved in such a way? He would have hated it as much as she had done. He would have been angry, throwing the same kinds of harsh words in her direction as she had done at him. And then at the end of it all, he would have smiled at her, holding his arms wide in an endearing gesture of submission. Inevitably. It was the way he had ended half a dozen minor disagreements they had had.

But then he would have put out a hand to pull his companion close to him, he would have transferred his smile to the dark head nestling in his arm, just against his heart. 'You mustn't be angry with me, Krista.' And her body would have obligingly melted for him. 'Not on the night that Barbe and I have become engaged. I insist that all my friends should be as lyrically happy as I am at this moment.'

And then, of course, in her lacerating imaginings she had been excluded, forgotten as he and Barbe gazed at each other.

'Mademoiselle.' The deferential voice of the chauffeur was a welcome intrusion into her painful thoughts, and she jumped out of the car as soon as she realised he was looking at her with an anxious expression. Krista bit her lip and raised a hand to brush away a tear which was stinging her cheek, convincing herself that he could have noticed nothing.

But when she was in the fast train to Paris her thoughts could not help returning to what had happened. What would Ludovic think when he discovered that she had gone? Barbe promised she would make some excuse, but surely it would have been more honest to tell him herself that she wanted to go home.

And it was hard to believe he would let her go, just like that. During the two hours she had to wait at the airport she kept expecting to hear her name being called over the loudspeaker system. Once or twice she caught sight of a dark head in the crowds that milled about her, she got used to the feeling of her heart bounding in her chest, then the anguish when the head turned and she found herself looking at a total stranger.

Even when she reached the top of the aircraft steps she could not resist a backward glance, hoping that she might see him waving wildly among the clusters of friends and relatives. But they were too far away to be able to distinguish faces. Besides, she knew that he hadn't come. He would be too angry with her. Angry but somehow relieved.

It was strange getting out of the taxi at the front door of Traquhair Lodge. Strange seeing the pile of cases the driver had desposited beside her on the steps, strange to ring the doorbell, to wait with hammering heart and clammy hands for the shadowy outline behind the glazed panels of the door, then for the door to be opened.

The split second before Mrs Meikle recognised her told Krista more explicitly than anything else could have done just how unexpected her arrival was.

'Krista!' At least the pleasure was genuine enough as the door was thrown back and the housekeeper bent to help with cases. 'My goodness, this is a surprise! And you having to ring the doorbell!'

'I didn't have the key, Mrs Meikle.' The tremulous smile might have been the result of coming home. 'I left it behind when I went away. I'm sorry if I disturbed you.'

'Of course you didn't. Bessie and I were just putting up the net curtains in your aunt's bedrooms. We've taken advantage of the opportunity to wash them.'

'The opportunity?' As they walked together up the stairs the girl turned an enquiring face to the woman she had known all her life. 'What opportunity is that, Mrs Meikle?'

'Och, surely you haven't forgotten, Krista?' The woman's smiling face said that she expected to be contradicted. 'Your aunt's gone off on her cruise, my dear. She left yesterday. And she won't be back for three weeks.' She threw open the door of the pretty pink and white bedroom and led the way inside. 'Now before you do another thing I'm going down to make a wee cup of tea for all of us. Come down to the kitchen as soon as you like and you can tell us all about your travels.'

It was only when she was alone again that Krista allowed a huge sigh of relief to escape her. Not for worlds would she have told Mrs Meikle that she had been right in her first assumption. The recollection that her aunt was due to set off with Mrs Dalrymple-Shand on a cruise taking in Madeira and the Azores had completely slipped her mind.

But now she could relax. Mrs Meikle and Bessie would be less probing than Lady James and it would be easy enough to explain to their satisfaction her erratic behaviour. Now she had three weeks in which to decide what to do. By the time her aunt came back from her holiday she would have a story off and be word-perfect. And most important of all, it was long enough for her to get over her infatuation with Ludovic Hasek.

'Well, it's nice to have you back again, my dear.

Whatever the reason.' While Bessie had been with them, listening enthralled to Krista's slightly exaggerated account of her adventures since leaving Scotland, Mrs Meikle had seemed prepared to accept the reasons she had given for her premature return. But now that the younger woman had gone back to hanging the curtains upstairs, the housekeeper was prepared to show some disapproval. 'But I think it was a bit unreasonable of Mr Hasek to tell you just like that about his secretary returning.'

'Oh, it wasn't like that.' In an effort to hide the colour in her cheeks Krista began to gather up the cups and saucers, walking with them across the immaculate blue and white tiled floor to the sink. 'He didn't suggest that I go. I just suddenly felt a bit homesick and wanted to leave. And now,' she looked out over the garden, bathed in the golden light of the late summer sunshine, 'now I wonder how I managed to stay away so long.'

'Hmm.' Mrs Meikle was not to be so easily convinced. 'I was never in agreement in the first place. Not that anyone asked me for my advice.' She spoke with all the authority of someone who feels free to offer an opinion without being asked. 'It was all done before I knew anything about it. Gadding all over the place when you've a perfectly good home to stay in!' She took a tea towel and began drying the dishes Krista was rinsing, affording herself an ideal opportunity to study the girl's face. 'You're sure you're not feeling ill, Krista? You look a wee bit peaky.'

'No, of course not.' It was an uneasy laugh. Could a broken heart be described as an illness? Most likely it couldn't. 'No,' she shook her head with what she hoped passed for conviction, 'I'm just a bit tired, that's all. I was up early this morning to catch the plane.'

'Well then, you just go on up and unpack. Then you can lie down for an hour before I make something for us to eat.'

'Well, don't go to any trouble, Mrs Meikle. I'll have whatever you're having. I don't feel hungry.' Determined to avoid further questions, Krista walked firmly towards the door, but was forced to pause before she could escape.

'Oh,' when Krista swung round the housekeeper was very busy folding the tea towel, 'Mr Melville has rung once or twice—the last time just on Wednesday.'

'Iain?' Krista felt embarrassed by the housekeeper's searching look. 'I wonder what he wanted.'

'He was wondering how you were getting on, that's all. Asked me if I had any idea when you'd be back. I told him no, not knowing then what I know now. Maybe you could give him a ring some time.'

'Oh yes, perhaps I will.' She turned to go, but was stopped again.

'Have you two had a quarrel, is that it?' Mrs Meikle's voice had softened considerably.

'No, not really. Not at all.' She smiled, hoping it would be enough to bring the conversation to a satisfactory conclusion. 'There never was anything between us. Not anything serious.'

'Maybe not on your side. But you could do a lot worse, you know.' Mrs Meikle finished what she was doing at the sink and came across the room towards the girl. 'You know I'm fond of you, Krista. And I was fond of your mother before you.' The unexpected reference to her mother brought a sting of tears to the girl's eyes and she turned away, biting her lip. 'And I don't like seeing you like this.'

'Like what?' The words were thick, half-strangulated.

'You look unhappy. It's more than just being tired.' A hand came out and pressed the girl's shoulder in an unusual expression of emotion. 'Anyway,' she sighed, 'I can see you don't want to talk about it. But,' she hesitated, 'I was forgetting,' the affectionate hand dropped, she resumed her normal matter-of-fact voice, 'Anne Kennedy rang as well.'

'Anne?' With an effort Krista thrust emotions aside. 'It's ages since I heard from her. I wonder what she wants.'

'Oh, I can tell you that.' Mrs Meikle walked back to the window, 'she was asking if you would like to share a flat with her. Apparently she's left her husband and she's trying to find someone to go in with her.'

'Oh?' Suddenly all kinds of possibilities filled Krista's mind, possibilities which would take her mind off her present worries.

'And,' the tone made clear that Mrs Meikle had correctly interpreted Krista's reaction, 'I hope you'll think well before you go into any arrangements with her, Krista.' She spoke as if she regretted passing on the information. 'You know how unreliable she's always been. She's as likely to go back to her husband if it suits her. Then you'll be left and you'll be responsible for a high rent.'

'Of course I won't rush into anything.' But as she made her way slowly upstairs Krista's mind was busy with the idea. She would have to get a job, of course. But she thought she could find something. She, through her aunt, had lots of contacts and several people had over the past year or two suggested she might like to work for them. She had good shorthand and typing, at least she would have if she brushed them up, and she was good at organising things, much better after her short spell with Ludovic. Misery twisted her inside as she opened the door and walked across to the high window of her bedroom.

She missed him, quite desperately. And she knew that if she didn't do something pretty positive to occupy her time, she would go out of her mind. Besides, she couldn't bear to return to the comfortable but undeniably boring life of pre-Hasek days.

And that was another problem. She had been confident enough that she could fool Mrs Meikle—too confident, as the probing questions had clearly indicated. So it was a safe enough bet that Lady James would brush aside all explanations in her determination to get at the truth. Krista knew she would not be able to stand up to the cross-examination, so the only course was to introduce a diversion. Moving out of Traquhair Lodge to join forces with someone as erratic as Anne Kennedy would be just that. Besides, Anne was fun. If anyone could cure Krista of her depression, then that person was Anne. She would get her number from Mrs Meikle and ring her. Although naturally she wasn't going to rush into anything.

Anne had changed—that much Krista realised at their first meeting. She seemed to have lost much of her old bounce and sometimes, when the conversation lapsed, a dreamy, almost wistful look would come into her eyes, a look which told Krista she was less blasé and dogmatic about her coming divorce than she liked to pretend. In fact she was not the daring, slightly scatty girl who had been the scourge of the rather conservative ladies' college which they had both attended.

But she was so anxious to have Krista as a flatmate that the decision was made before there was time to consider the matter properly. Not that Krista had any regrets once she had given her promise. Anne was keen to solve her problems. And that made two of them.

Besides, it was such a lovely flat. No one, not even Lady James, could complain about it, for it was in one of the capital's fine Regency terraces and had been left to Anne by her grandmother.

'It's not so much that I can't afford to run it on my own, Krista.' The shrug and smile took some of the strain from her face, reminded her companion of the sixteen-year-old she had been. 'Only I don't want to be alone all the time. Besides,' she turned to hide her face, 'the parents are going spare. If you come to stay with me they'll cool down a bit. Mum always thought you were a good influence on me.'

'Oh dear!' Although Krista tried to laugh, the remark did less than nothing for her own self-esteem. 'That makes me sound middle-aged and sensible!'

'Sorry.' Anne was too immersed in her own thoughts to pay much attention to Krista's feelings. 'They seem to imagine that once I'm on my own I'll be living a wild life, forgetting who I am. But with you here, Krista, they'll know I'm leading a blameless life.'

'Thank you again.' She tried to ignore the pain that her friend's words had brought.

'Oh, Krista!' At last it seemed to penetrate Anne's mind that perhaps her words had been less than tactful and she turned round with an apologetic smile. 'I'm sorry, really I am. I just said *they* thought you were like that. I don't. If I did I can assure you that I wouldn't be all that keen to share with you. Besides,' her blue eyes studied the girl sitting opposite her with a new interest, 'there's something different about you. It's not just your looks. Although,' brutal frankness had been one of her less endearing qualities, 'no one at school would have thought you would be the one to turn into a beauty. And,' she brushed aside Krista's protest with an impatient hand, 'one with such style. But there's something else. I can't say what it is, unless . . .' a glint of understanding came into her expression, '. . . unless you had . . . Have you had a love affair, Krista? Something that didn't work out?'

'Of course not.' Krista was becoming adept at turning away from searching eyes.

'Oh well, if you don't want to talk about it I'm the last person to blame you. I feel exactly the same myself.'

'But you,' inside Krista's head she screamed the words, 'you at least know what it's like to be loved. Whereas I,' recollection of the night she and Ludo had gone to the disco filled her mind, once again she was standing by the open door of her bedroom, waiting for him to come in, 'I doubt if I would have the courage to take love if it had been offered to me. Only of course it wasn't. Ludovic never had the slightest inclination that way.' Before the torture of that silent admission could be too prolonged she became conscious of Anne continuing.

'I know so much about broken hearts myself,' there was a bitterness in the voice that jarred, momentarily diverting Krista from her own sorrow, 'that I feel I'm something of an expert. I can recognise the symptoms in other people and even if they manage to cover it up I swear I can smell unhappiness. That's why I know about you, Krista.' Her smile was slightly apologetic now. 'I can't begin to guess what it was, but I'm sure something happened when you were going about Europe with Ludovic Hasek.'

'You think so?' Deliberately Krista turned away, denying her friend any confirmation which might have shown in her eyes. 'Well, as you say, I did move around a bit, so the opportunities for romance were limitless. I may even have fallen in love with someone behind the Iron Curtain. It happens, you know.'

'Mmm. Well, I won't pry any more. I did think at one time that you and Iain Melville might make a go of it but . . .'

'We were just good friends.' Krista was determined to relieve the tension in the atmosphere, to try to lighten things for her friend's sake as much as for her own.

'Oh yeah?' To her relief Anne smiled a little. 'Believe me, Krista, there's no such relationship between a man and a woman. Anyway,' she too seemed anxious to veer away from the painfully personal, 'when do you think you'll be able to move in? I was hoping you might make it on Monday.'

'Oh no, I can't. I told you, Anne, not till my aunt has come back. I couldn't move out while she's on holiday—I owe her some consideration.'

'Well, I would have thought you'd repaid that years ago. She's depended on you too much. I still can't quite believe that she agreed to your going off with that conductor.'

Krista giggled. 'Sounds as if he's on the buses!'

'Well, you know me—no intellectual,' Anne

responded with a faint smile. 'Whose idea was it that you should go?'

'It was my aunt's.' It was a problem she had often posed, one to which she had not found a satisfactory answer. 'At least, when Ludovic made the suggestion she was only too happy to agree.'

'Well, in that case she can hardly complain now that you want to get off on your own. You're the only girl I know who's stayed at home all these years. Lady James just doesn't know how lucky she's been, with an unpaid companion always on call.'

'It hasn't been entirely like that,' Krista was forced to defend. 'She and Uncle Colin were always very good to me. I don't know what I would have done if they hadn't taken me in when Mum was killed.'

'Yes. But your uncle was different—he was a darling. But your aunt is inclined to be a bit ... domineering. In the nicest possible way, of course.' Anne's smile robbed the words of any unkindness.

'Maybe a little.' It was impossible for anyone to deny Lady James's strong personality and Anne's words forced Krista to remember the kind of life that was waiting for her at Traquhair Lodge. Safe, secure, dull, a round of commitee meetings and bridge parties which might satisfy her when she reached middle age but which she certainly was not ready to accept now. 'Anyway,' for the first time she felt total confidence in the course of action she was adopting, 'I'll begin to move my things over the weekend. That should be enough to convince you that I won't change my mind. And I have this interview on Monday, so ...'

'Is that the one at the airport?'

'Yes. Assistant to the personnel manager of Self-Drive. It's not a particularly brilliant job, but they want someone who can start in ten days, so I feel optimistic. And Mr Prentice says there are prospects.'

'Oh, good.' There was a touch of sarcasm in the other girl's voice. 'Does that mean by the time you're forty you'll have worked your way up to director?'

Suddenly the thought of being in the same job for years ahead chilled Krista and she shivered slightly. 'Something like that,' she said.

Gradually her bedroom at her aunt's house lost its personality as all the little bits and pieces began to disappear from the tables and dressing table, one or two flower prints were removed from the walls and cases filled with clothes were taken along to the flat. Mrs Meikle noted everything with a disapproving air, although after having said her piece on the subject she managed to hold her tongue.

On the Saturday night when Krista came back from the flat she was too tired to notice the strange look given her by the housekeeper, but the less critical manner gradually percolated through her exhaustion. Gratefully she accepted the cup of tea which was thrust into her hand when she went into the kitchen and sighed as she sank down on to the chair.

'You know, Krista, I *do* understand why you're so keen to get away from home.'

'You do?' At once her senses were alert, the thick fringe of lashes flicked up, allowing the dark grey eyes to study the older woman keenly.

'Yes.' Mrs Meikle, apparently a little disturbed, got up and crossed to the cooker where she fidgeted with a pot for a second or two. 'I know perfectly well.'

Heart hammering, Krista waited without speaking.

'I know it must be boring for you with just older folks for company.' The housekeeper returned to the table and sat down opposite Krista, apparently unaware of the feeling of relief that suffused the girl. She had thought for a heart-stopping moment that somehow Mrs Meikle had discovered her secret. 'And maybe,' Mrs Meikle, unusually diffident, went on, 'I've been against your moving in with Anne just because I'll miss you such a lot if you leave. You see,' she almost apologised, 'it's nice for me when you're in the house, Krista. It hasn't been the same since you went away. And now you're thinking of going for good . . .' Her eyes were suspiciously bright. 'I was just being selfish, feeling sorry for myself.'

'Oh, Mrs Meikle,' absurdly touched, Krista reached out a hand towards the other's, 'I'm sorry. But it isn't as if I'm going to be miles away from you. I'll be over two or three times a week. If Aunt Diana wants me,' she qualified with an intensified feeling of anxiety.

'Of course she'll want you.' Briskly Mrs Meikle thrust aside any tendency to sentimentality, squeezed the girl's fingers and stood up again with uncharacteristic restlessness. 'Why shouldn't she want you? But . . .' she hesitated with one hand on the teapot, which stood warmly wrapped in its blue and pink knitted cosy on the table, '. . . I'm trying to tell you, Krista, that I've done something a bit silly.'

'Silly?' Krista frowned, smiled in disbelief and shook her head. 'That I just can't believe. But tell me what you've done. Get it off your chest.'

'The truth is, I've asked someone along for supper tonight.' She fingered a gold brooch which she often wore at the neck of her blouse.

'Well, why on earth shouldn't you? This is your home and you know your friends are always welcome.'

'Oh no, not for me. For you, Krista.'

Her first inclination was—oh no! Not tonight. Not when I want simply to lie for an hour in a hot bath, then have a sandwich and a cup of coffee in front of the television. Then the idea of Iain Melville came into her mind and she remembered Mrs Meikle telling her that he had rung several times when she had been away. 'Oh, Mrs Meikle . . .' Irritation began to give way to anger.

'Yes, I know I shouldn't have done it. Only I felt so sorry for him. He'd been here twice when your aunt was away from home and then when he came this morning, he seemed lonely. And he hasn't made any friends here, so . . .'

'Just who—who on earth are you talking about, Mrs Meikle?'

'The new minister. Well, the assistant, I suppose I should say. You knew that young Mr Brodie had got a church of his own and that he and his fiancée have moved up to Balmaha. They're being married there next week, I understand.'

'The new minister?' Relief that the supper guest was not to be Iain Melville softened Krista's reaction to the idea of having to abandon her plans for a restful evening. 'What's his name, Mrs Meikle?'

There was an instant's hesitation before the reply, hasty and embarrassed, came. 'Oh, it's . . . Johnston. Paul Johnston. It was just that I felt so sorry for him, Krista.'

'Oh, it's all right.' Krista stood up, yawned and stretched. 'I don't mind, not really. And besides, I don't suppose he'll be waiting very late. Not if he has his sermon to prepare for tomorrow.'

'Well, I don't know about that.' Mrs Meikle's relief seemed slightly exaggerated. The minister and to a lesser extent the assistant were frequent visitors at the Lodge and it was natural enough for Mrs Meikle to have issued an invitation. 'But I'm sure he'll enjoy some young company.'

'Right. I think I'll go up and have a bath now. I'm tired after all that humping about. I didn't know moving could be so exhausting. What time did you ask him to come, Mrs Meikle?'

'Oh, about seven.' She was very busy clattering pots in a cupboard. 'Now you go along. I'll have to get busy and make him something nice to eat. I don't suppose he gets much in the way of treats, living in the flat at the Manse. I know Molly Cameron is always hoping the assistant will be married, then she won't have to bother.'

There was a faint smile on Krista's face as she ran up the broad, luxuriously carpeted staircase. Although Mrs Meikle was very friendly with the housekeeper at the Manse she was never slow to remind everyone that cooking was not Mrs Cameron's strong point. Cleaning, yes. The rambling old manse always gleamed with the results of her elbow grease. Sew, yes. The sitting-room positively glowed with all the birds and bouquets of flowers she had embroidered on cushion covers and chairbacks. But she was a reluctant and not very competent cook.

As she lay soaking in the hot scented water, Krista wondered idly what the new minister would be like. There had been a succession of young men over the years, at least one of whom, Lady James declared in the skittish way guaranteed to put paid to any possible romance, had the intention of carrying off her niece. Fortunately he had seemed to Krista not the least bit like Young Lochinvar and she had been able to put up with the teasing without any ill effects.

And she knew, without the shadow of a doubt, that tonight's guest would be unlikely to cause the merest ripple of anything approaching interest. There was only one man who could do that, and he was miles away. By this time he might even be married. She imagined that once Barbe had got the engagement ring on her finger she would not feel safe until a plain band had joined it. The thought caused a lump to rise in her throat and she got out of the bath without even thinking of using the soap.

There was a feeling of relief in her mind as she applied herself to the task of getting ready. Her first inclination was to throw on any old thing, but then a vague kind of yearning, a longing to see an expression of admiration in a man's—any man's—eyes made her riffle through the remaining clothes in her wardrobe a second time.

And she chose a blouse, the filmy white one she had bought in Vienna, or rather Ludovic had bought it for her, which she had been saving for a special occasion. The special occasion which had never come. The morning, golden and happy, when they had wandered along a tiny narrow street of elegant boutiques would not be blotted from her mind. They had been celebrating a particularly successful, joyful concert the previous evening, both of them still slightly drunk with the ecstatic response from the audience.

Krista had pressed her nose against the glass, admiring the delicate garment negligently displayed in the window against a background of black velvet. A few scarlet roses were scattered on the floor of the window.

'It would suit you.' Ludovic persuaded as he lounged against the wall, his eyes on her face rather than on the blouse.

'Oh, of course I can't. It would be hideously expensive.'

'What else is money for but for buying what we want?'

'Mmm.' She began to walk on. 'I don't think . . .'

'But I think, Krista.' The lithe dark-clad figure stopped with his hand on the door latch, holding it open so that a bell rang, continued to ring so long as he stood there.

'Ludovic!' she protested, with a guilty frown towards the dark interior of the shop.

'I shall stay here until you make up your mind. Hurry, Krista.' He pretended to be severe. 'You are causing a disturbance.'

'Well . . .' She hesitated, attracted as much by his lightness of manner as much as the gorgeous blouse.

'Come then, *drágám*.' He pushed the door a fraction so that the insistent ringing stopped and she caught sight of the saleswoman hovering in the splendid showroom, all black and scarlet with touches of dull gold.

And when she had tried it on, displaying it to his critical eye with a return of the shyness she would have sworn she had overcome, he had insisted that she should have it, brushing aside her attempts to pay with smiling impatience.

'You shouldn't have!' When they had completed the purchase they stood in the quiet alley, Ludovic grinning down at her, holding the gold and black package teasingly by its string.

'I know, I know. Only I could never resist giving presents to beautiful young women.' And to add to her confused pleasure he hummed a few bars of the waltz from *Der Rosenkavalier*, the music which had been received with such rapture the night before.

And she, little imagining that before she had the opportunity to wear the delicate thing they would have parted in anger, had floated two feet above the ground for the rest of the day.

She only hoped that the minister would approve. If he didn't then he must be very hard to please indeed. So Krista consoled herself as she put the finishing touches to her make-up. Discretion had been her theme, for the bloom of summer still clung to her skin, all it needed was a touch of blusher to her cheekbones, a smear of apricot lip-gloss and she was ready.

The skirt she was wearing, a deep rose-coloured silk jersey, swirled about her legs when she walked, but its simple lines threw into contrast the sheer pintucking of the blouse, the high collar, long sleeves and deep cuffs contradicting the sensuous glowing quality of the white silk. She would do, she decided tucking a straying strand of hair beneath the black bandeau which held it piled on top of her head. But when it immediately escaped she didn't trouble to touch it again. Already she had gone to too much trouble—all for the assistant minister, a man she hadn't even met. As she ran downstairs, resentment against both him and Mrs Meikle for being the cause of so much trouble rose inside her.

'He's here.' An unusually nervous woman was waiting for her when she reached the hall, and Krista raised an eyebrow in surprise when she saw the two patches of colour on Mrs Meikle's cheeks. 'I just put him in the drawing room. There's a fire on there—in case he's feeling the cold,' she explained.

'Do you think he will be?' For some reason the conversation seemed to be making little sense to Krista.

'What?' Mrs Meikle spoke in a whisper.

'Do you think he'll be feeling the cold?'

'Oh well,' the colour on the cheeks grew deeper if anything, 'it's beginning to get a wee bit nippy at night.'

'I would have thought if he could stand the manse he could stand anything.' Her resentment was beginning to show, so to soften the words she tried to smile. 'What did you say his name was?' She paused with her fingers firmly on the handle of the drawing room door.

'Jackson. Mr Jackson.'

'His first name, I mean. But . . . I thought you said he was called Johnston.'

'No, you must have misunderstood me, Krista.' Now she was simply mouthing the words. 'Paul Jackson. Oh, and I won't serve the meal till you ring. It will keep for as long as you like. Nothing will spoil.'

Krista frowned questioningly at the housekeeper, who suddenly turned and, in total contradiction of her words, rushed back towards the kitchen. There was still a puzzled expression in her eyes as she pushed open the door of the drawing room and went inside.

He was standing by the French windows, just as he had been on the day when he had asked her to go away with him. And now as then, he held a think black cigar between his teeth. His eyes were narrowed against the plume of blue smoke as it rose in the air and she saw his fingers go up, take it from his mouth and crush it out in the large crystal ashtray which was kept on top of the grand piano.

His eyes, those strange dark eyes, reached out and touched her—her hair, her mouth, moving to the filmy whiteness of her blouse, then returning to linger this time on her mouth.

'Krista!' She had forgotten the possessive power with which he was capable of investing that single word. Forgotten what it was like to struggle against the throb of her own senses which even now were threatening to overwhelm her with their insistent message. *'Drágám!'* The voice became even more sensually potent and he took a step towards her, the dark hands reaching out.

'Ludovic!' It was an effort to keep the right amount of amused lightness in her voice, but she succeeded beyond her wildest dreams. She drew a deep breath, quelling with a ruthless determination the sob that started deep in her throat. And she was helped by the rage that came in a great wave, engulfing all her foolish tendency to a more tender emotion. How dared he. How *dared* he! Ignore her for all this time and then play this cheap trick on her!

'Ludovic.' Confidence flowed back into her and she was able to add a brittle laugh to the coolness of her manner as she repeated his name. Her eyes held his proudly and the change in his expression, a hardening, a sudden sweeping away of gentleness, thrilled her with a feeling of power.

What a surprise to see you when I came down expecting to see the minister. Those were the words she intended to speak, and they would be accompanied by a casual turning away as she went over to the cabinet to fuss about with some drinks.

But to her dismay the dark face now so close to her began to blur and grow dim, she felt as if all the blood was ebbing from her head and heart,

there was a fierce sting of tears behind her eyes
and the words that came from her lips were not
the ones she had in mind.

'Tell me,' even her voice was not her own, 'how
is your fiancée? Or perhaps by this time Barbe is
your wife?'

CHAPTER TEN

THE words hung vaguely about the room, seeming to have immobilised both of them but as suddenly as it had come Krista felt all the anger drift away from her, so she was left empty and spent. So long as he makes no attempt to touch me, she thought, I'll be able to hang on to some self-control. But then she remembered the meal which even now Mrs Meikle might be dishing up in the kitchen and she knew how impossible it would be for her to sit opposite him and to hide everything of her feelings.

At last she saw his lips move and he spoke. But his words had nothing to do with the question she had thrown at him.

'Why did you run away, Krista?' If he seemed a trifle paler, slightly strained, it was just a trick of the light or perhaps even a comforting illusion with which she could console herself. Yet his eyes were dark as ever, persuasive, encouraging, infinitely to be feared. She forced herself towards the action she had intended earlier and with a condescending smile turned towards the drinks cabinet. While she had her back towards him she could feel his eyes boring into her. 'Why, Krista?' The timbre had changed, he had hardened towards her and for the first time there was a harsh note in his voice, demanding an answer.

'Why?' she asked lightly while her hands on the sherry decanter shook. 'Because I didn't think I should be missed.' She turned round, a crystal glass in each hand, her face suddenly blazing with indignation. 'We'd come to the end of the season, had we not?'

'And do you think . . .' He strode towards her, took the glasses from her fingers with such force that the liquid spilled, she felt the warm stickiness on her wrist. There was anger, barely controlled, in the way he banged down the glasses and turned to face her again. In the depths of his eyes something she had almost forgotten sparkled, some emotion that made her shiver. Dark hands reached out for her shoulders, merciless fingers cut into her tender flesh as he shook her. 'Do you think that is all there is to be said on the matter?'

'What else?' With a defiance she had not known she possessed she glared up at him. 'I can't have been missed so much or you would have contacted me before.' All the bruised feelings, the damaged emotions from his failure to do that stung again with painful rawness. 'For all you knew I could have been murdered . . . or anything.' Self-pity added to her anguish. 'For all you cared!'

'So . . .' he hissed at her, his lips drawn back over his teeth, 'still you think so very little of me.' He shook her again before releasing her with a contemptuous gesture. 'If that is so,' there was a bleakness about his mouth as he turned away from her, 'there is nothing we can say to each other.'

Krista whirled away in a fury, biting her lip to save herself from the humiliation of tears, and at the same time she was arrested by his reflection in a mirror, arrested and betrayingly struck by the weariness in his manner. In a moment all her bitterness and anger were swept away in the tidal wave of love, tender, sympathetic, melting. She longed for nothing more than to put her arms round him, to hold him close to her, to comfort him as she herself longed for comfort. And yet her wounds were too fresh to risk further laceration. Forcing herself with a little sobbing sigh, she turned again, her mind finding that other question to which she had as yet received no answer.

'How is Barbe?'

It was a moment before he looked up at her, another before he understood what she had asked. 'Barbe?' The shake of his head was minimal. 'She is well—I believe so.'

There was something about his words, about the way they were uttered, dispassionate, detached, as if her query had neither interest nor relevance for either of them that caused a flutter, deep down, almost imperceptible in her senses. Just then she was too confused, too bewildered to understand why she should feel such a positive lightening of her spirits, only life seemed, for the first time in weeks, something to be viewed with a modicum of hope.

But suddenly, as if to contradict her Ludovic took her by the shoulders again with the same fierceness as before but without shaking her. The dark blue eyes blazed down at her with an expression she had never seen before. Yes, she had—once or twice, but so fleetingly that she had not dared believe the evidence of her own eyes.

Now her heart was hammering against her ribs, there was an urgency in her blood which demanded a response from him. And as if he sensed that need his voice grew gentler, less brutal, infinitely more seductive.

'What did you say to me?' The strongly marked eyebrows were drawn together in a frown, but there was nothing accusing in his manner, rather it was puzzled as if he was trying to explain to himself why he had not heard her first words. 'Krista—*drágám*.' At the endearment, the throbbing quality of his voice, liquid fire pulsed through her veins. 'What did you say to me when first . . .' now his mouth was very close to her face, his breath was warm against her, the scent of his cologne, familiar, distinctive mingled with cigar smoke in her nostrils.

'When . . .' She was bemused, unable to think when his eyes were being so distracting.

'When you came into the room, *drágám*? What was that question you asked me?' He smiled, briefly but with sudden brilliance. 'For I swear the words are in my mind and I cannot believe you really spoke them.'

'I asked——' now his mouth was so close to hers that she could feel his skin on hers when she spoke, 'I asked——' her voice quavered, broke.

'Did you ask, or perhaps I am only dreaming it, something about my fiancée? And Barbe?'

'Yes.' She dared not move, dared not interrupt the delicious closeness.

'My God!' It was part laugh, part cry of despair, but at the same time he pulled her against him, roughly, tenderly, folding her close, resting his cheek on the top of her head. 'My God!' he repeated wearily. 'Is this what it has all been about? *Drágám*,' he held her away from him, laughter behind the fatigue on his face as he gazed down at her, 'dare I hope you were perhaps a little jealous of Barbe?'

'Of course not,' she said, and burst into tears.

It was a positive release to weep. Half lying, half sitting on the sofa with his arms wrapped about her, his mouth against her hair while he murmured comforting words in languages she didn't understand, she almost enjoyed it. Only when she realised that not only had she soaked his handkerchief, but the immaculate dark grey jacket

was distinctly damp and probably his shirt and tie
as well, only then could she force herself to stop.

'Oh dear!' Refusing to look at him, she dabbed
ineffectually at his lapels with the handkerchief,
then, merely to check, slipped her hand inside his
jacket and against his chest where she could feel
his heart beating almost as rapidly as her own.

At once it was captured, held there. 'You see?'
He shook his head as if he were as much
bewildered by his emotions as she. 'You see what
you are doing to me, *drágám*?' He took a tress of
her hair, wound it round his finger, pressed it
against his lips while his eyes, filled with heady
tantalising promises, refused to release hers.

'I must look awful.' Her mouth was trembling
and she caught her lower lip sharply between her
teeth and struggled to sit up.

'You look beautiful, *kedvenc*. I mean to spend
quite some time over the years telling you how
beautiful you are.' Krista was scarcely able to
consider the heady implications as he went on,
'But now, first of all you must tell me what you
meant by saying Barbe and I were to marry.' He
frowned in perplexed amusement. 'How could you
think such a thing, Krista?'

Only for a second did the possibility of
concocting some story flit through her mind,
something which would protect the woman they
were discussing. Then she realised that this above
all was a time for truth. 'Barbe told me so.'

The fingers which had been tracing tiny
tantalising arcs at the nape of her neck were
suddenly stilled, he frowned down at her as if he
had misheard. 'Barbe . . . told you . . . what?'

'She told me that you and she were to be
married.'

'So!' The word was a hissing accusation and the

dark blue of his eyes shone with an icy
implacability, as he muttered some words in his
own tongue. 'I would not have believed it of her.'

'And,' Krista's voice quavered with the possibility that perhaps he did not want to believe it,
'she told me that you no longer wanted me to act
as your secretary.' The time hadn't yet come when
she could let him know exactly how cruel and
bitter the Comtesse had been; perhaps later, she
dared hope, later there would be time. 'She said
you didn't like to ask me to go and that it would
be best if I simply left.'

'Krista!' His face twisted. 'And you believe this.
How could you?'

Suddenly miserable that she was such an
obvious disappointment, she bit her lip and looked
away, only to find her chin caught and turned
forcefully in his direction again.

'I . . . I don't know, Ludovic. Perhaps—perhaps
it was because I couldn't quite understand why
you chose me in the first place.' Her expressive
grey eyes were hidden from his view by the sweep
of long thick lashes. 'I've always wondered . . .'

'I too,' his voice now shook with such
suppressed laughter so that she could not resist an
upward glance. 'I too have often wondered,
Krista.' Her name on his lips sent the familiar
throbbing surge through her body. 'It was not
until that day we played truant, that day we
escaped on to the beach, that I began to
understand the true answer.'

Now there was only one place to look, and that
was directly into his eyes. Yet when she did, all her
normal sensibilities seemed to drift away from her
and all she could think of was . . .

'It was only that night, when I had gone to my
room in the *auberge*, do you remember, Krista?'

He held her even closer for an instant and laughed into her face. 'You should not say such things, *drágám*. Not unless you wish to have your bedroom door tested in the early hours of the morning. When I lay in bed, all I could think of was you and I wondered, could it be possible that you had meant to invite me to share your bed? That's why I came along to your door later to see if you had left it open. You hadn't, and I decided my first understanding was the correct one.'

Krista felt her colour increase, laughed rather selfconsciously and looked down at her fingers. 'If I'd known . . .

'Perhaps, *drágám*,' he nibbled at her ear lobe, 'perhaps it is as well you didn't. I should have hated if I had had to spend the rest of my life feeling guilty about that.'

'The rest of you life?' Seductively she traced the curve of his cheek with her fingers. 'What do you mean?'

'Later.' He caught her fingers and touched them to his lips. 'I shall tell you what I mean later. Now I want to ask you about Duclos. Have you any idea how I felt when I saw you in his arms? I hope you did it only to make me jealous.'

'No, no,' she denied passionately, 'of course I didn't! That first night at the Cheval Blanc he came over to me and asked if he could join me. Afterwards I wondered . . .' At this moment it seemed a bit mean to express her suspicions, but Ludovic continued for her, in a voice that had more than a touch of cynicism.

'You wondered if he had been sent specially to pick you up there.'

'Yes, I don't know if . . .'

'Of course it was so.' His eyebrows drew together angrily. 'I am sorry, Krista—I should

have seen what was happening. It was only when I
saw Jean-Paul and he said something that I began
to suspect a little of what had been going on. I still
can hardly believe that Barbe would be so devious.
I know that she and Duclos had an affair once, a
long time ago when her husband was alive.'

'Did she tell you that?'

'No, of course not. She does not even know that
I'm aware of their relationship. But that was one
of the reasons why I was concerned when I
thought you were becoming fond of him.'

'But I wasn't. I wasn't!' It seemed essential that
he should be made forcibly aware of that fact.

'Yes.' He spoke softly, rubbed his chin against
her cheek so she could feel the faint stubble of his
chin. 'Yes, I know that now, *drágám*. But at the
time I did not. I simply saw you becoming more
involved than I liked with a man who was totally
unsuitable for you.'

'But . . .'

'And if you care to ask why he is unsuitable
then I shall be forced to tell you that I consider I
am the only man who is suitable for you.'

'When did you first think that?' Krista hoped a
conversation along these present lines would go on
all night.

'When Duclos was on the scene. I disliked him
for the reasons I have explained, but also because I
had never before suffered the tortures of raging
jealousy. It was some time before I was able to
identify it completely.'

'So now you know how I felt when Barbe told
me you and she were to become engaged.'

'You were jealous, *kedvenc*?' His arms tried to
strain her even closer to him.

'Mmm,' she said, and brushed her lips dreamily
against his.

'You had no need,' he said huskily. 'There never was anything between us. I've known Barbe for many years, since I met Jean-Paul when he was first at the Conservatoire. At that time we were all struggling young musicians and Barbe was on the look-out for a rich husband. She found one, but although she got what she wanted I don't think she was any happier when she was rich than when she was poor. She had a miserable life with Sebastian and it was only when he died that she had any of the freedom she used to enjoy. I have felt sorry for her, estranged from her family because of her marriage, with a great deal of money and very little else. Not even a child to enjoy. Now . . . she must be totally warped to have told you such a story. There was no question of my marrying her, even before you came on the scene. But you know,' he looked down into her face, blue eyes searching hers with an intensity that made her quiver with the urgency of her response, 'you still haven't told me that you will.'

'That I will . . . what?' She held her breath, smiled when he looked down at her with an expression of lighthearted amusement.

'You are right, *drágám*,' to her surprise Ludovic rose to his feet, swirling her round in an arc before depositing her on the floor in front of him, 'these things must be done properly.' With a gentle finger he touched the filmy white material of her blouse where it filled out with the curve of her breast. 'I'm glad you wore my gift to you, Krista. I swear that even then I was beginning to have thoughts about you, entirely inconsistent with any I had in mind when I took you away from your aunt.'

'Yes.' She was very conscious that their only contact was through that casual finger at her breast, aware that it was driving the breath from her body, causing her heart to become even more agitated and insistent. 'And still I don't know why. Why you wanted to take me away from . . . the . . . from my aunt,' she finished with a touch of mischief.

'I can see I'm never to be allowed to forget that phrase.' His eyes sparkled in response. 'But I forbid you to mention it again. As to why I asked you to take Jerzy's place, I couldn't have explained it myself at the time. I know only that it became an obsession. I had to bribe your aunt outrageously before she would even allow me to approach you.'

'Bribe her?' There was incredulity in her voice. 'My aunt?'

'To tell the truth, I'm not certain whether she blackmailed me or if I bribed her. Only the final result is the same. I'm to conduct a charity performance of the City Orchestra for one of her hospital charities. Oh, she's a very businesslike woman, your aunt. She knows only too well how to strike a bargain. Then,' he gave a faint laugh, 'when the proposition was put to you, it was turned down flat. I found you a very opinionated, trying young woman that afternoon.'

Remembering something, Krista giggled suddenly, then bit her lip in an effort at self-control.

'Tell me what is so amusing,' he demanded.

'It's so hilarious. I don't know what you'll say.'

'Go on.' The strange eyes narrowed, although the smile was still on his lips.

'That afternoon, when Aunt Diana said you had something to tell me, it crossed my mind that you and she were to be married.'

'You . . . what?' His grimace of disbelief was comical. 'You thought that Lady James and I . . .'

'. . . were to be married.' Her voice trailed away.

'So, first I am to marry Lady James.' It was impossible for her to decide whether or not he was amused. Perhaps he would be so insulted that. . . . 'Then I am to marry the Comtesse du Boulet. So many widows and titles to choose from! And all the time,' his arm suddenly snaked out and pulled her hard against his body, 'all this time, I have been longing to ask if you will be my wife. Now you must answer me. I cannot bear to wait any longer.'

'Do you,' she reached up a hand to stroke his cheek, 'do you really need to ask?'

'I hope I do not.' His eyes sparkled in sudden amusement. 'But if the answer is no, then I swear I shall enter a monastery. If I cannot have you then I shall leave the world and all its pleasures behind me. Tell me, Krista.' In impetuous insistence he seized her hand, holding the palm against his mouth. 'I am asking you to marry me.'

'Of course I'll marry you.' She spoke so softly he had to bow his head to catch the words. 'It's all I've been thinking of since I first met you, don't you know that?'

'Kedvenc!' His eyes closed in a brief gesture of relief and satisfaction and he sighed. 'If I had known that, my life over the last weeks would have been so much easier. How soon can we be married? If we make all the arrangements perhaps the ceremony could take place as soon as your aunt returns from her cruise and . . .'

'How did you know she'd gone off?' Krista was certain there had been no mention of her aunt's movements. 'I'd forgotten all about it until I came home.'

'I know because I rang Mrs Meikle on the day after you did your flit. At first I was so angry with you, and with Barbe, that I was determined to cut you out of my life completely. But then the next day I had to phone and find out how you were. Mrs Meikle said nothing about it?'

Krista shook her head. 'Not a word.'

'I asked her not to. I told her that I would be coming over within a few days. And then I had a call from California and had to fly across there on an emergency. That is what has kept me from you. So, you see, it isn't quite true that I did not care what happened to you. At least . . .' he hesitated teasingly.

'At least . . .' she prompted with an appearance of pique.

'At least not after that first day. Then I swore to myself that it was hopeless, that I would have to learn to live without you. But soon I realised just how impossible that would be. And that,' his lips brushed disturbingly against hers, 'that is why I'm determined to marry you as soon as possible. Do you think we can have everything arranged before Lady James comes back?'

'I think . . .' she began, although it was becoming increasingly difficult to do just that with his mouth so close to hers, 'I think . . . maybe we could try and . . .' She gave up the struggle, yielded to the exquisite pleasures invading her senses.

'Darling!' Ludovic whispered on a sigh. 'It must be so, otherwise . . . I should hate to have Lady James suspect me of seducing her niece, especially if it were true. I should feel very guilty, knowing how carefully she had brought you up.'

'Ludovic!' Krista protested, but mildly.

'It's true, my sweet.' He laughed down at her, then the smile faded as his attention was drawn to the lips parted so invitingly. 'But now . . . just before we go and confess to Mrs Meikle that you've decided to marry the minister, there's something I must do.'

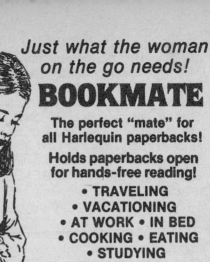
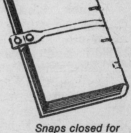